Hera: To C

S. M. Ca

Copyright 2023 © S. M. Campbell
All Rights Reserved
ISBN: 9798373044967

I

The sky was a soft azure, dotted with clouds still reflecting the early morning lilacs and blushes and golds cast on them by the suns. There were likely a myriad ships beyond that peaceful atmosphere, gliding amongst the stars and flashing neon lights of spaceports, one step closer to the goddesses who had birthed the galaxy.

But Rynn's eyes were on the ground: the swaying of young green shoots of grass, the lazy shifting of the tree branches, and the breeze that seemed to link the foliage into the same gentle dance of the day's beginning. He glanced at the slender deer that pulled his grandfather's cart and at the garden it was grazing next to that spilled over and out onto the grass. His eyes then drifted to the tiny cottage where he lived with his grandfather.

A small ladybug crawled across his limp hand. Its shell was black, with two prominent spots of red, like drops of blood amongst ink. Rynn stared at it, at the same time noticing how the energy inside of him had grown increasingly frenetic lately. It had first started out as a small fizz, and then sparked up, and crackled and spat so impatiently Rynn felt he could almost *hear* his veins buzzing.

The ladybug lifted its shell and then its wings carried it away from Rynn's finger. He stared after it, an uneasy feeling coming to his stomach. He felt the blades of grass bend to caress his neck. The wind seemed to change direction, and it now ruffled his hair and cooled his skin.

He heard footsteps, the crunching of leaves distant but growing nearer.

Suddenly his eyes shot open. Confused, he blinked and rubbed them. Had he been asleep? He had a tendency to grow distant and stare at the woods bordering his home for hours—but this time he snapped out of his trance, even his energy seemed to have shorted.

But he had indeed heard footsteps. His eyes fell from the tops of the trees to his grandfather, who was laden with multiple bulging bags. Rynn sprang up and rushed over to the old man.

Asold Hera had a gray beard, long hair, and something in his eyes: some twinkle that was usually dim, but when Rynn caught sight of it, it seemed as if the old man knew something. The twinkle served to disturb Rynn, but only whenever he detected it.

"What did you harvest?" Rynn took some of the pouches from his grandfather's arms.

"Tomatoes, carrots, cucumbers, lettuce… All the excess can be sold in town." The old man said it with a wary tone and squinted in the midmorning sunlight.

Rynn fumbled with the bags and his eyes caught on the staff tied behind Asold's back—a staff with a unique head of blades. It was the staff his suspicious, alert grandfather always carried, along with his paranoid demeanor. Rynn could not understand what could possibly unsettle him.

"Grandfather…" Rynn began, stopping as he noticed the twinkle in Asold's eyes.

They entered the quaint cottage, and the supplies crowded the main room. Rynn's grandfather removed the long leather jacket covering his everyday robe. He then set to unpacking a few of the sacks' contents to be washed, his movements a little stiff.

Two bright red tomatoes emerged, along with a bundle of carrots, and Asold headed for the basin.

"Grandfather," said Rynn again, pausing when Asold glanced at him, "I was wondering if you would let me go into town with you next time."

His grandfather said nothing and proceeded to wash the vegetables.

"The festival is coming up. You always come back with so many stories. They make me wanna visit more and more every year."

Asold dropped the cleaned vegetables into a stained iron pot and then looked at Rynn. "We've discussed this, boy. The town is not safe, especially during the festival when all those skeptical merchants come in."

"But you can't just keep me here forever! Why won't you let me go into town?" Rynn could sense the routine argument materializing.

"Because you're young and there are a lot of people there who are…" He seemed to mull over his words before settling on "…trying to hide from the law."

"I'm not *that* young," Rynn muttered, feeling impatient. Asold abandoned the food and walked over to Rynn. "Please, child, if you understood why we live so far away from the town, you wouldn't ask to leave."

Rynn perked up. That was as much information as his grandfather had ever betrayed, as close as Rynn had ever come to comprehending the knowing twinkle in Asold's eyes.

"Now please help me wash these."

Rynn glanced around and then obeyed, still troubled.

• • •

That evening they ate in silence, though Rynn's mind was loud and chaotic. His extremities tingled and threatened to burn the entire length of his arms and legs. He squirmed in his seat, causing Asold to turn his head.

The old man then glanced at his staff, which was propped against the wall, its blades catching the white light of the rising moons that streamed in through the window.

Rynn's skin suddenly became clammy, and he stood. He looked at Asold. "May I be excused?"

He only half waited for the man to nod before making his way out of the small house and into the cold night air.

He lifted his head and stared at the empire of blinking stars that had revealed themselves in the cover of night, the domain of the goddesses. He had heard every tale of how the seven sisters, daughters of a star, had made a long journey to the void that was now the galaxy Rynn resided in and each birthed a planet she would protect forever after; he had heard of how they once dwelt amongst mortals and even ruled them as their queens; and yet he never tired of hearing them again, or looking up into the sky and wondering if they were looking at him as well.

His grandfather had taught him he was to be immensely grateful to the goddesses and all of the sacrifices they had made, all of the ambrosial blood—for Rynn had been told it was sweet to taste—their veins had likely shed. When Rynn had asked what sort of sacrifices, Asold only explained that he was too young for such tragedies.

The five moons gazed down at him and cast an eerie light on everything surrounding him. A breeze rustled the trees' leaves and crept beneath Rynn's clothes and a chill spread across his flesh. There was a peculiar humming in his ears.

Rynn felt a hand on his back and jumped, startled. He turned to see his grandfather. He deserted the old man and sat on the steps leading up to the cottage's door. Asold stood close by. No words passed between them, though in the warm light that spilled out from the house's windows, Rynn could see his grandfather was thinking.

Rynn, too, was thinking. He was confused by his grandfather's ever-present caution, and had been forever. What was there, really, that Rynn needed protection from? Although he had to admit to himself that he, too, had been uneasy lately. It was as if some great monster lurked in the woods surrounding Rynn and his home, never attacking but always watching.

"I trust you," Rynn said finally.

Asold stroked his beard. "And it is I who must also trust you." There was a long pause, then: "I will let you come into town with me for the festival. But only once."

Rynn could not help the smile that blossomed across his face. He moved to slide off of the steps. Standing, he approached his grandfather.

"Thank you, Grandfather!" He embraced the old man, who stared absently into the sky at all of the stars.

II

Rynn watched as his grandfather fastened his staff to his back. The suns had just risen, filling the house with a soft lavender glow, and Asold had explained they needed to reach the town earlier than some, for though the settlement was not extremely far from the woods surrounding their home, they were required to present the vegetables for sale before the actual festival began.

Asold still seemed stiff, wary. A very small part of Rynn felt rueful for finally getting what his grandfather had for so long resisted, but the entire remainder of his body was filled with excitement at the prospect of something different, something new.

They had hitched Asold's wagon to their harnessed deer and Asold assisted Rynn in seating himself atop the tall cart. Asold himself did not mount the cart. Instead, from within the folds of his jacket and robe, he produced a thin dagger and sheath and held it up to Rynn.

Rynn took it cautiously and studied the silver blade, which bore an ethereal pastel glow in the cold, misty morning. A chill crept through his hands and arms. He frowned at Asold. "Why…"

The old man interrupted him. "As I explained, town is dangerous."

He then climbed onto the cart beside Rynn, jolting the reins before the deer carried them onward.

・・・

The town came into view once the suns were directly overhead—a small assemblage of stone buildings standing in a weathered council amongst the towering fir trees.

Rynn's ears filled with the lively chorus of the town. Everyone was out of their homes for the festival of Arsteine's patron goddess Kazari: animals were being herded through the main square, booths were being erected, and multiple carts besides that of Rynn and his grandfather's were also pulling into the commotion. Eventually it all seemed a mere hum to Rynn, however, for his veins had begun their queer pulsing again.

Something made him turn and stare into the smudged, cloudy windows that the cart was passing. Several pairs of critical eyes stared back. Rynn's lips parted as he grew distant, the eyes still glowing behind the filthy glass.

The cart hit a pothole in the cobblestone street and Rynn lurched forward, shaken from his stupor. His arms and thighs tingled. He began to bounce his leg.

He glanced around the town and drank in the most people he had seen in his entire life. The majority were merchants or farmers from further reaches of the kingdom who, with their tents, had extended the town by a few leagues.

Towns all across Arsteine would be celebrating Kazari and the existence of the planet, and in his stories Asold had told Rynn of the celebration in the capital city: in the day, games and an endless flow of honeyed kebabs and candied fruits; the waving of colorful flags and ribbons and confetti; and in the evening a candlelight homage display and bursting fireworks. He had told Rynn not to hope for such extravagance in a town as small as theirs, but that the villagers still felt just as or more grateful and full of respect for Kazari.

Asold halted the cart and helped Rynn down, instructing him not to leave his sight. Rynn watched as a group of women arranged strings of wildflowers on the booths and the buildings encircling the festival, the fragrance of the blossoms drifting delicately through the fresh midday air. Several merchants placed small devices on the counters of their booths which then lit up and displayed holographic advertisements and menus.

Several girls in homemade flower crowns rushed past him. A wagon full of hay wheeled past. Rynn made his way through the crowd of diverse festivalgoers, shoving past a few idle villagers, his arms hanging limp at his side though they crackled with the strange energy he could never pinpoint. A few very young children, younger than Rynn, sang a hymn he was unfamiliar with. A tall figure brushed past Rynn. The energy inside of Rynn suddenly dissipated, but somehow he felt even more feverish than before. It caused him to stop for a moment, in a daze. The tall man, too, had paused. He looked into Rynn's wide gaze with two troubled blue eyes. Rynn stepped out of the way of a festivalgoer and when he turned back around the man had vanished.

Soon Rynn stood leaning against the old well in the center of the town, perturbed at his accelerated heartbeat and flustered mood. He had just begun to study his grandfather, who was unloading the cart, when a group of five boys dressed in dusty, worn robes who looked around Rynn's age confronted him.

One of them stepped forward, a youth with disheveled brown hair and an odd chip in his ear. "Hey," he said, "I haven't seen you here before. Are you with one of the merchants?"

Rynn's eyes scanned the group. "No, I live a little ways out of town," he replied.

The boy grunted. "Wanna play with us?"

"Um…All right."

A few of the boys chuckled.

Another boy, this one with dark red hair, grasped the arm of the first boy as he began shifting excitedly along with the others. "Here. You can be the emperor." He placed a crude crown fashioned out of twigs on top of Rynn's head.

The emperor. Rynn, confused, adjusted the makeshift crown on his head and then waited to see what the group would do next.

The boy with the split ear pulled a stout stick out of the belt around his robe. The red-haired boy also brandished a stick and all of the others followed suit. Rynn took a step back.

The first boy glanced around, and then to the others said, "Not here. Follow me. You too, Emperor Dusek."

"What?" Rynn furrowed his brow as the group led him to an alley formed by two wildflower-clad houses.

"*Now* attack him," the boy with the split ear, evidently the leader, ordered.

All of the boys began circling Rynn, chanting obscenities about the emperor he did not understand, though they recited them as if they were the most time-honored of adages. One of the boys carried a peculiar banner with an even queerer symbol upon it, which he soon let fall to the ground, causing the other boys to trample it.

"Get him! He denounced the celestialists!" cried the lead boy.

"What does that mean?" asked one of his accomplices.

"I don't know, I heard my parents say it."

At once Rynn felt a hard thump at his side. He glanced between all of the boys, armed with sticks and an unsettling expression across all of their faces indicating that to them this game was innocent play. Somehow one of the many sticks managed to painfully strike his eye.

Suddenly he remembered the knife his grandfather had given him and went to yank it from its sheath just as he felt another blow from one of the sticks.

Quickly, he held his dagger out towards the boys. Their eyes widened and they backed away slowly.

"He has a real sword!" one of them cried, causing the others to retreat.

Once he had been deserted, Rynn gingerly sheathed the dagger and rubbed his smarting eye. The previously ignored wounds also cried out as he left the alley and uneasily trotted back to the square. Soon he spotted his grandfather conversing with a man standing with a cart of melons.

Remembering Asold's order to remain near to him, Rynn quickly took his place by his grandfather's side.

"…could probably sell them for a little more than that," the stranger was telling Asold. Asold grunted and then the man paused. "This your lad?"

"My grandson," Asold replied, turning to Rynn. He definitely noticed the faint bruising around his eye, for his eyes widened at the boy before quickly kneeling in front of him. As he gripped Rynn's shoulders, his eyes were sparkling with something akin to fear. In a gruff voice, he asked, "Are you bleeding?"

Rynn shook his head, mute as he studied the anxiety on his grandfather's face.

Asold slowly rose to his feet and apologized to the man, brushing his hands off on his robe.

"Very nice," the man said curtly. "Now anyway…"

The words that passed between the two adults became a muffled hum to Rynn's ears. A bizarre feeling fluttered in his stomach, and he examined the town and the festival that was commencing.

Rynn celebrated Kazari's fair, though not without the strangest of dizzy, distant sensations. He had the feeling that he was being watched by every member of the village and every visiting merchant, as if he were a lame fawn girded by starving wolves.

Rynn and Asold participated in every merry custom the festival entailed, including the throwing of flower petals, the enjoying of highly sugared candies, and the ritual of lighting the candles in honor of the patron goddess. However, even as they did, Rynn had the subtle notion that some of the merchants and villagers were unfriendly and unscrupulous, although he constantly shoved the idea away and out of his mind, intent on enjoying the moment he had so desired to experience.

He hoped to relay his thanks to his grandfather, to show Asold how joyous he was that the old man trusted him enough to bring him to the place considered to be such a grim shadow for so long. But his grandfather seemed wary, throughout the entire festival stiff and alert and glancing about.

Finally the day reached its end—though most of the merchants had left their booths, the townspeople still celebrated even with the coming of dusk—and Rynn and Asold returned to their now-empty vegetable cart and Rynn, arms full with a small basket of sweet cakes, set to chattering about how much he loved the town, and about Kazari, and how he did not understand why Asold had not brought him to the village sooner.

The setting suns cast a warm, dappled glow the same color as the candied peach slices Rynn had eaten earlier in the day through the canopy of trees that lined the crude path Asold used to return to their cottage. The wagon jolted them often.

"This was probably the best day for me to come to town with you," Rynn told his grandfather contentedly.

"Yes..." Asold sounded perturbed. He cleared his throat and gripped the reins harder in his hands.

Rynn tried to analyze him in an attempt to figure out what was causing him to be even more unsettled than usual.

His grandfather accelerated the cart's speed.

Rynn, confused, turned to question his grandfather, but was silenced by the urgent, almost fearful look etched into the man's wrinkled face. The cart's pace increased yet again, and Rynn thought he could see, in between the violet-tinted trees lit up by the dying trio of suns, several shapes moving like shadows amongst the forest's own natural ghouls.

Soon the familiar copse came into view, but Rynn was anxiously watching their pursuers, for pursuers they were. One of them leapt from the shelter of the woods and onto the cart in a scarlet-tipped black blur. They brandished a long, scythe-like weapon and sunk the blade into the soft body of Asold's deer, goring the animal and causing it to collapse on the ground in a writhing fit. The cart began to veer, now having no guide.

The shadow also slashed at Rynn before oddly running off to rejoin the others.

He felt a sudden sharp, intensely painful blow to his upper arm as the black metal dug into his flesh. He cried out and watched as his grandfather grabbed his staff and barely brought the cart to a halt before leaping off of it and running up to the violent figure.

Asold managed to sink one of his staff's blades into an unidentified part of the shadow, but then looked back to Rynn.

"Run! Get out of here *now*!"

The trepidation in his grandfather's voice threatened to freeze Rynn right where he stood.

"No! I—"

"Go!" It seemed the only word the man's mouth could form.

Rynn abandoned any hesitation as he turned and bounded for the cottage that had been reduced to a mere smudge amongst all of the other dismal purples of the quickly approaching night.

The ground was a speeding gray blur beneath his feet. Rynn should have been puzzled by the ambush but the danger made his mind spin and he had forgotten everything but escaping, surviving.

He hardly noticed the screaming pain in his arm and he nearly tripped over his own feet. What would have been a tranquil, silent evening was disrupted by the abnormally loud thud of his heart in his throat, the sound flooding his ears. The cottage lay before him and he raced up to the door.

Rynn grabbed the doorknob and shook it frantically, hands trembling. The door opened and he fell into the house and onto the wooden floor. He stood, and after bolting the door shut he made for the window, where he plastered his hands and nose as his eyes desperately sought out the shape of his grandfather emerging from the dark line of trees.

Soon Rynn saw Asold running for the cottage just as he had a few moments ago, though Asold knew who the strangers were and so fear a thousand times more potent defaced him. As the elderly man neared the house the shadows caught up with him, overtaking him in an instant.

Asold stared back at the house, and for a moment Rynn believed they had actually made eye contact. But then a curved, black blade erupted from his grandfather's chest and instantly the familiar sand-colored robe was scarlet with gore.

The old man crumpled to the ground and Rynn froze, cemented to the floor by the window. His lips parted and he exhaled, causing a fog to bloom across the frosted glass. For the first time Rynn could clearly make out every shadow that had been a part of the ambush.

There were seven of them: seven strangers wearing peculiar white and red masks, and hoods bearing a crimson triangle, otherwise garbed in black from head to toe and each holding a long, curved sword or some type of scythe. Rynn stared at the place in the grass where he had seen his grandfather fall and swallowed hard.

He immediately tore away from the window and darted towards the small closet in the furthest corner of the house. He buried himself beneath ancient wooden crates and worn robes just as old. His breath hitched. He heard the heavy falling of footsteps and not too far after the thudding of fists or weapons on the door.

They were going to kill him. They had already gashed him and stabbed his grandfather, and now they were going to kill him.

He attempted to keep himself from crying as he clamped a hand over his mouth in the darkness of the closet. His brow creased and his chest heaved anyway. He squeezed his eyes shut and tried to smother the blind fear. Suddenly there was a thud as the strangers, the *creatures*, finally managed to bust down the wooden door.

He heard muffled voices.
Someone choked.
A grunt.
Groaning.

Silence.

Rynn's muscles were taut and quivering. His face was buried in his knees and he was begging Kazari to protect him.

And suddenly the entire house was completely silent. The only sound Rynn heard besides his wild heartbeat was the almost cautious footsteps approaching the very closet he was hiding in. Rynn's heart pounded in his ears and his veins began to burn. He was finally conscious of the searing pain in his arm caused by the curved blade of one of the masked strangers.

The door creaked as it swung open and allowed a stream of moonlight to grace the dark closet with its soft glow. But then the glow was disrupted by a shadow that sliced through the previously ethereal light.

Despite himself, Rynn peeked through his fingers to get a glimpse of the thing standing before him.

For an instant he believed one of the murderous intruders had discovered him curled up in the cramped space. The figure standing before him was a man dressed in black, like the strangers—but unlike the strangers he wore no outlandish painted mask, merely a black veil over his nose and mouth. A pair of pristine, bright blue eyes gazed in an almost lamblike manner into Rynn's frightened, large brown ones. They were flooded with some overwhelming emotion the boy could not identify.

"Who—Who are you?" Rynn asked, his voice quivering.

The man blinked but did not move. "A friend." He held out his hand to Rynn.

Rynn's eyes caught on the dark bodies lying on the floor of the cottage and then he looked back up at the man. He bashfully took the hand offered to him and was pulled out of the uncomfortable hiding place.

The two of them stood in silence for what seemed an agonizingly long time, until finally Rynn felt obliged to speak to the man who he now viewed as his rescuer. "Well…whoever you are, thank you. We were on our way home when those people ambushed me and my grandfather…" Something painfully struck his chest. "My grandfather!"

Rynn broke into a run and abandoned the friendly stranger and the cottage-turned-morgue to race across the gently swaying meadow in the cold night air. "Grandfather! Grandfather, where are you?" His eyes found an oddity in the grass and he ran towards it.

Asold was lying in the grass, the gloom of night making his robe appear to be covered in ink rather than clotted blood. His gray hair was a silver spray around his face. His eyes still shone with the last sparks of life.

Rynn bent at his side. "What should I do? Grandfather! I don't know what to do!" Tears freely made their escape down his cheeks.

Asold sighed. Rynn refused to look at the gaping hole in his abdomen. "Rynn…"

Rynn bent to Asold's lips.

"You have to listen to me. You…You have to run." The words were barely voiced; they were a mere gasp for breath.

"How do I save you?" He took Asold's hand in his.

The old man used his other wrinkled, shaking hand to reach for Rynn's wounded arm. As he gazed at the limb, the smallest of smiles cracked his lips before disappearing as quickly as it had come. "You have to get away from here. You have to listen…" His eyes grew distant, as if he were somewhere far, far away—for he was.

"Grandfather?" Rynn bent over the body and clutched the wrinkled robes in his fists. He felt lightheaded, and his veins pulsed in the queerest manner they ever had.

After sitting in the grass beside his grandfather, head bowed, he reluctantly stood and glanced around at the meadow. He sought out and found Asold's multiple-bladed staff, though somehow a good portion of its stock had been snapped off. It was now the perfect size for him to wield. Rynn gripped the shortened weapon for a heartbeat and then began gathering every leaf, every flower, and every weed to cover his grandfather with, causing a disruption in the previously serene ocean of grass with the jumbled assortment. Rynn blinked and the tears that had been welling up in his eyes fell in rivulets down his face. He sank to the ground beside his grandfather and began to sob.

The stars hung overhead in a solemn assembly, as if the goddesses themselves were honoring the passing of Asold Hera into their world and comforting Rynn, if only by their cold, distant twinkling.

15

III

Rynn felt as if he had been sitting there beside the makeshift burial for eons, still as a marble statue and just as solemn. He heard footsteps making their way through the grass and out of the corner of his eye he saw the stranger, the young man who had saved him, approaching. The tall grass swirled around his hips. He halted a few feet from the boy and his deceased grandfather and Rynn could feel the man's gaze boring into his spine.

Rynn sat back on his heels and wiped his nose with the loose sleeve of his robe. As he did so, a sharp stinging wracked his upper arm. He had completely forgotten about his wound, relatively small in size, where one of the murderers had sliced him. He dared to look down at the injury, and his eyes were met with a gaping abyss, far deeper than he had thought it would be. His pale sleeve was splotched with blood, but it did not appear ordinary. It had an unmistakable luster to it, so that it almost glistered as if it contained ultra-fine crystals. It also seemed to emit some strange afterglow even though some of it had already dried and caked around Rynn's wound.

He screamed and stumbled backwards, nearly falling to the ground. He had seen his grandfather's blood whenever he had nicked himself with a knife or pair of pliers, and the blood that flowed from Asold was definitely not anything like whatever flowed from Rynn's arm.

"My blood! What's wrong with it? What's going on?" He turned to see the stranger, his veil gone and his entire face visible. His lips were pressed into a firm line and his eyes were still flooded with the unfamiliar emotion.

Rynn abruptly stood and stared at the man. He was still as a gloved hand reached for his arm and examined it. The man sighed.

"The goddesses," he muttered.

Rynn frowned. "What?"

"You know of the seven celestial goddesses?"

Rynn nodded, and in the man's voice he could identify the accent of those who lived in the innermost parts of the capital—the same as his grandfather.

"You carry their blood in your veins. You are offspring of one of them."

Rynn's eyes widened and he stepped away from the man. "What? How would you know?"

"I only know how to use my eyes," he replied. He gestured at Rynn's arm. "Is it sweet?"

"You want me to—to *taste* it?"

The man stared at him.

Rynn cringed and then, as painlessly as he could manage, dabbed the tip of his finger into the wound. He sucked the blood from his fingertip and the taste was made evident. It was indeed sweet—syrupy, almost—and caused his tongue to tingle. Suddenly his mouth became unusually dry and Rynn began coughing.

When the fit subsided, he said, "I don't understand…"

He found himself face to face with the piercing, pale blue eyes again. "You are the forbidden son of a goddess and a mortal. Because of this, you must heed your grandfather's advice and leave this kingdom, this *planet,* now."

"Are you suggesting my grandfather *knew* about my blood?"

"It's possible. Now please, we need to leave now."

"I don't even know you. How do I know I can I trust you?"

"You don't. But if you do, I promise I can keep you safe, protect you. I know somewhere we can go."

Rynn's shoulders sagged and he looked back at the patch of grass where his grandfather now rested and then at the house, which suddenly appeared so empty. He lifted his head to see the stranger and then took a step towards him. "All right. Please help me."

• • •

Rynn followed the man through the woods, and as they trudged across the leaf-covered ground he thought he could make out the shapes of the town's buildings through the gaps in the trees. The suns were rising and softly illuminating the landscape with a cold, pale glow.

They rose just as they had the day before, as if nothing had changed. As if Asold was not dead. As if Rynn was not a descendant of one of the celestial goddesses, who were the daughters of a star.

The fact frightened him, for what would be expected of him now that he knew he had something very close to liquid power flowing beneath his flesh into every single part of his body? Clearly others knew of this, or the assassins would not have come after him. The slender fingers of a tree branch brushed the top of his head and Rynn started. He glanced at the wound on his arm. In the light of the swiftly arriving morning the blood seemed to sparkle even more.

The man, almost merging with the gloomy contours of the forest, turned back to look upon Rynn with an almost sympathetic look that was visible only in his eyes—for anywhere else on his face always remained neutral and as unchanging as a painted portrait. "The ship isn't too far now," he murmured.

And soon they reached it. A small, black, sleek but beaten starship, Rynn wondered why he had not seen it enter the atmosphere or heard it land. It sat in the midst of a clearing in the woods, a bit ominous and very foreign amongst the familiar swaying trees and dappled ground.

The man grasped Rynn's uninjured arm and helped him into the ship. Marveling at the fighter ship, for he had never seen one so close let alone been inside of one, Rynn glanced around at its interior, which consisted of an empty main area that led to a ramp and a doorway. It was a bit larger on the inside than he had perceived from without.

"Why is it so torn up?" Rynn asked.

"I crashed it a few times when I was learning how to fly it," came the muttered reply.

"Where did you get this thing?"

The man did not respond as he lowered his hood, revealing a mane of dark brown hair that almost curled, and instead made his way to the doorway at the end of the hallway into what Rynn recognized as the cockpit.

He examined it even as the stranger bade him take his seat in the copilot's chair and he slowly obeyed. He watched as the gloved hands darted across all of the control panels and flipped multiple switches. The cockpit was then illuminated by numerous indication lights.

Rynn studied the view of the forest at daybreak from within the slightly rounded window of the canopy. The ship lurched, throwing him forward.

"Buckle your seatbelt," the man ordered.

Rynn complied.

The ship thudded again and then lifted gently into the air, whereupon the young man pointed its nose skyward and and steadily pushed a lever, which accelerated the ship.

Unknowingly, Rynn gripped the arms of his chair as the trees became minuscule dots and the clouds and rising suns seemed a thousand times nearer than they ever had in his lifetime.

The sky was breathtaking, a panorama of blushing clouds and fading stars surrounding a fulvous bloom induced by the pale, young morning suns. The sunrise further illuminated the cockpit and cast an idyllic light upon the young stranger's hair and pitch-black garb, and Rynn looked down at his own hands to see he, too, was infected with the same glow.

They left the sunrise behind far too quickly, joining the gradually dimming stars that still bobbed in the gloomy gray-blue ocean of last night's tragedy. It, too, was stunning—albeit in a melancholy, musing, almost mournful way. It reminded Rynn very well that he was about to leave all he knew behind and break through the atmosphere into the vast expanse of nothing that lie beyond it. He looked over at the man, his pale blue eyes reflecting the light of the few stars that fought their daily demise.

"What's your name?" Rynn asked.

"My name is Kilderan," he said diffidently, almost a whisper, as if he were afraid to utter his own designation.

"I'm Rynn," Rynn said.

Kilderan looked at him as a torrent of wispy clouds blazed past the cockpit window. "Nice to meet you…Rynn."

Rynn smiled for the first time in a while and settled deeper into his chair. His veins throbbed after being calm for so long. The pain in his arm awakened as well, and he asked, "Why do we need to leave?"

It was a few long moments before Kilderan answered. When he did, he seemed as if he had just returned from somewhere very distant. "The emperor," he said. "He was somehow affiliated with the goddesses and that is how he discovered the celestial blood and its properties. We have to leave because if he was to find out about you, Rynn, he would do horrible things to you in order to extract what he is after."

"I thought the emperor was a good man." Rynn furrowed his brow. Slowly, he asked, "What would he use it for?"

"Your blood is basically a drug, and he's addicted to it. He wants what it can give him—power, immortality… anything that can aid him in keeping his hold on the galaxy."

Rynn considered his words, though he was unsure what he was supposed to say. Then he turned to Kilderan. "Why did you offer to protect me in the first place?"

Again, it was several heartbeats before he answered. "I knew those assassins were coming after you. I just wanted to help." He looked over at Rynn as the ship thudded. "And now, even more so because of the fact that you carry the celestial blood." He scanned Rynn, the boy's tattered, sand-colored tunic with one crimson sleeve; his grass-stained trousers; his slightly ruffled, sandy blonde hair; and then queried, "How did you even end up in the middle of the countryside, the son of a goddess?"

Rynn turned back to the window. "I don't know. I didn't even know I had the celestial blood until last night. My grandfather and I have always lived out there." His breath hitched. He leaned forward and felt odd when the region all around the ship was nothing but space: cold and dark and dotted with tiny pinpricks of light from the stars, with no indication of what was up or down or left or right.

"Carefully," Kilderan said, "If you go to the back of the ship, you can see Arsteine through the window."

Rynn unbuckled the seatbelt across his chest and made his way towards the small porthole at the end of the short hallway.

Amidst even more of the black void Arsteine hung like a suspended marble—a marble that was slightly periwinkle blue mingling with white spirals and glowing against the inky scenery. It was absolutely breathtaking, and Rynn stared at it for several moments, trying to match the landscape that was so familiar with the otherworldly orb that seemed almost ominous in its elegance.

Soon Rynn deserted the window once even more distance was created between himself and the planet. He returned to his seat in the cockpit. "Where do you come from? What were you doing before you met me?"

"I'm from Thruhairth."

Arsteine's capital, Rynn thought, the fantasy of the gleaming city during Kazari's festival filling his mind.

"Were you close with your grandfather?" Kilderan asked suddenly.

"He raised me." After a silent moment, Rynn added, "He never wanted me to leave the woods. He told me it was dangerous." He folded his hands in his lap, glancing at Asold's staff propped against the wall of the ship.

"You're fortunate to have someone who really cared about you," Kilderan said in a low voice.

"I—" Rynn blinked and altered his reply. "Do you have any family?"

Kilderan stared for a long, long while at the window. Finally, he said, "I have a brother."

"Really?"

Still drifting through the distant world of thought, Kilderan continued, "He and I haven't spoken for a very, very long while."

"Oh," Rynn said rather dumbly.

Kilderan tore his gaze from the window and settled it instead on Rynn. "No—That isn't what I meant. I would relish the chance to speak with him."

Without warning the ship lurched and accelerated, turning the still sky around them to streaks of blurred stars and suns. Rynn watched as Kilderan released the ship's controls and turned his chair towards Rynn.

Rynn gazed at the tunnel of light they now sped through and then began, "I'm so confused now, though. Everything feels so empty and lonely and…" He swallowed and then blinked at Kilderan. "And I have the blood of the *stars*. I don't know what I'm supposed to do. I did back on Arsteine, with my grandfather…" He felt immature for having tears fill his eyes for what he counted as the thousandth time that day.

Kilderan noticed his tears. "You aren't supposed to know. At all. I want you to know that I want to help you, I do. You don't understand how valuable your blood is to some, what they will put you through only to extract it." He grew absent as he cautiously reached for Rynn's hand and engulfed it in both of his. "You're very young, but I can tell that you are smart. Please trust me."

Rynn looked up into his eyes. "I—I do. But I still don't understand why you're so intent on protecting me."

"Like I said, your blood is valuable and if you were to fall into the wrong hands it would be terrible. I've seen the effect the celestial blood has on people." His eyes filled with something akin to the twinkle Rynn often noticed in Asold's eyes: as if he knew something.

Rynn was puzzled by the amount of sincerity Kilderan showed, for they were merely two strangers with no idea of one another. But he could tell the young man's words were honest: desperate, even. He scanned Kilderan's face. His eyes were filled with that now-familiar vague emotion, but his face seemed distant and wistful.

"Rynn, there's something—" Kilderan began.

Suddenly Rynn's veins began pulsing and pain screamed along the entire length of his arm. He hissed and clutched his upper arm, eyes watering.

Kilderan sat up and took Rynn's arm in both hands very delicately. He loosened the veil they had tied around it, revealing a small, shallow wound that gushed glistening blood in excess despite the injury's size and severity.

Rynn's brow creased and around his vision swirled a halo of starlight produced by the ship's jump through space.

"We need to stop the bleeding, before far too much of that blood gushes out. And it will." Kilderan stood abruptly from his seat and rushed to the back of the ship. "There's a closet back here…" He opened a door inset into the wall and Rynn leaned over the side of his chair to see a small compartment containing a few shelves.

Kilderan snatched two containers from the closet, immediately opening a red one. "Empty. Blast it." He began rifling through the other container and pulled out packets of stale sustenance paste and slightly cloudy water. "Isn't there anything in here?" Rynn heard him mumble. Then he pulled out a small ration heater and tugged his knife from its sheath.

Rynn turned his chair back towards the window and examined the abnormal-looking wound and its peculiar reaction to what should have been a minor abrasion.

He saw Kilderan approach out of the corner of his eye and then heard the man say, "Look away."

"What?"

Rynn felt a searing, scalding pain more intense than the first sensation and cried out. He looked down at Kilderan's knife pressing down on his flesh and yelled again. "What are you doing to me?"

Kilderan did not respond until the black dagger retreated into his sheath. "If you had bled out, it would have been worse than that." He produced a torn strip of fresh fabric and gestured for Rynn's arm, which the boy proffered.

Kilderan took his arm gingerly in his own hands and wrapped the injury.

After he was finished, Rynn clutched his arm and stared up at Kilderan, who had returned to the pilot's seat. *He seems to know far more about the celestial blood than I,* he thought.

The ship halted its rapid race across the ocean of stars startlingly quick and Rynn found himself face to face with a massive sweep of orange clouds and yellow splotches and swirls of green. As he reexamined it, he realized he was staring at a planet.

"Umeda," said Kilderan. "We're here."

IV

It was several minutes of flying towards the planet, which to Rynn looked like a painting with all its colors bleeding into one another, before they actually entered the atmosphere.

When they did, they found themselves floating above a seemingly endless field of delicately whipped clouds tinged with the soft golden light from the setting suns. The ship almost drifted along with the clouds in their own tranquil, unhurried fashion.

Rynn for a moment felt suspended in the air and held up by nothing but his sheer will. He watched the sky through the window, the wings of the ship brushing the clouds and creating swirls and wisps from the disturbance in the billows.

Kilderan flipped a few switches on the dashboard of the cockpit, initiating commands completely alien to Rynn, and then the small black fighter ship cut through the clouds and plunged into a simultaneously sunny and rainy setting above a city. On the horizon, Rynn spotted the looming shape of a palace, tinged a smokey blue in the sunset.

He heard the sound of thrusters amidst the buffets of wind and turned to Kilderan.

Rynn noticed a map on the cockpit's control panel. "Are those other ships?"

Kilderan nodded. "Hopefully they won't notice us."

Rynn perked up as the sound of crackling speakers emerged.

A dull voice spoke. "Attention spacecraft. We have been authorized to scan your vehicle. Please remain stationary."

Concern etched into his normally statuesque, expressionless features, Kilderan slightly accelerated the ship.

A sterile, masculine voice spoke. "Attention spacecraft. We have identified your vessel—" Another voice interrupted the first, this one more human. "—Prepare to relinquish all your valuables or risk being blasted out of the sky!" Every other fighter pilot on the channel chuckled at his melodramatic delivery.

The ship continued to accelerate. Kilderan swore. "Pirates."

The ship gave a loud thud and he swore again. "They just fired at us!"

Rynn sat forward in his seat. "Why? We didn't do anything!"

"Exactly." Kilderan glanced at the ship's dials and then pushed a lever. The city became a blurred mass beneath them.

Another blast struck the hull.

Rynn briefly looked through the window at the end of the ship and saw that three more of the pirate fighters had joined the pursuit. "What do we do?"

Rynn nearly got thrown from his chair as Kilderan swerved and aimed the ship towards the city. Rain ran in rivulets down the cockpit's window, streaking the glass with droplets in their own chase.

Rynn turned to the window once more and frowned, seeing that two fighters had vanished from the gang. He glanced at Kilderan, who seemed to notice nothing but whatever escape route he had decided upon for them. The ship grew closer to the ground.

The city was sprawled out beneath them, an assemblage of tall concrete houses and shops dotting the landscape in a seemingly random manner. The scenery had turned to a blur as Kilderan maneuvered the ship to evade the pirates, who were following close behind.

Kilderan directed the ship skyward and the city began to shrink. Partially veiled by the mist of the rain, the three suns blazed before them, filling every nook of the cockpit window and glaring in their faces. The ship changed direction and Rynn froze as they flew upside down and left behind their pursuers.

"Did we escape?" Rynn asked, his head spinning.

But then the small, battered ship came to an ungainly halt inside a ring of ramshackle ships. Rynn identified the previously missing crafts among them.

"Attention spacecraft. You are under arrest. Cooperation is suggested as you and your vessel are escorted to Umeda's moon, where you will be detained until—" The voice was interrupted again. "You're coming with us. I don't know why you thought running would be a good idea…"

Kilderan jammed his finger onto the comm button. "We don't have anything of any value!"

There was no reply.

The ship now flew at a greatly reduced pace, encircled by the fighter ships. "We *will* shoot down your vessel if you show any resistance," said one of the pilots.

Rynn turned to Kilderan. "They're taking us to the moon?" He swallowed and adjusted the belt on his robe. "What's gonna happen?"

"Calm down," he replied, his steely blue eyes boring into Rynn's face. "If we perform any further attempt to escape them then this will grow worse than it already is."

Rynn exhaled and his eyes scanned the young man sitting across from him: his black garb and the dainty earrings that glinted in the sunlight. Rynn squinted. He froze when Kilderan glanced in his direction, but he did not seem perturbed by Rynn's gawking.

Rynn's arm throbbed, and he grasped it. The ship continued to be ushered further into the sky and the air seemed thin. The full realization of being incarcerated finally settled into his head and sank into his mind. He began to worry what would become of him and his blood, for Kilderan's words had planted a fear inside of him, a fear of being hunted and killed for the ichor, and it was one he often nurtured.

Kilderan sat as one keeping a strict vigil, but his eyes darted around the scenery visible through the thick metal frame of the cockpit. Dust particles drifted in the air and threatened to alight on his dark eyelashes.

The smoky blue horizon now displayed a softly glowing moon, and its image burned itself into Rynn's vision. Although he had never been in space before meeting and fleeing with Kilderan, Rynn felt at ease and almost sedate whenever he was in the stars' presence. Perhaps it was because he now knew that his mother was closer than ever, that she was one of the coruscating ghosts hung in the sky. Perhaps it was because of Kilderan, who had brought him to this haven that seemed like a sanctuary where nothing could touch either of them nearly anywhere they went in the sky. He was definitely unsettled about their destination and about the reason they were escaping Arsteine in the first place, but some atmosphere that emanated from within Kilderan served to comfort him and in a way almost reminded him of his grandfather, the way he was very nearly desperate to protect Rynn.

Rynn felt a weight on his foot and froze, his musing also halted. His head snapped up and his eyes shot to Kilderan's dark boot on Rynn's own soft leather one and then to the boot's owner.

Kilderan seemed to twitch and almost recoil. "You were bouncing your leg," he explained. "You need to calm down. I'll get us out of this."

Rynn slowly nodded and then began to fiddle anxiously with the longest lock of his bangs.

• • •

The moon grew nearer and nearer and gradually its surface grew larger and larger as they approached. Rynn noticed a decently sized station of some kind surrounding the grey-blue satellite that seemed more like a minuscule planet to him. He watched Kilderan out of the corner of his eye.

The voice of the first pirate invaded their ship's speakers once more. "Head for the hangar with the blinking orange light inside it and land there," he ordered.

Kilderan obeyed without saying a word or, as far as Rynn could tell, even exhaling.

Soon the ship landed in its designated location with a heavy thud on the landing gear and Rynn glanced around, cold air nestling itself beneath his clothes and against his previously warm flesh.

Their captors had not broken their formation even as they, too, landed. Rynn stood and went to the window at the back of the ship. He turned back to Kilderan, only to start when the pitch black coat was all he could see as he nearly ran into Kilderan.

Rynn looked up at the man who towered over him, brow creasing, for never before had he noticed the small collection of scars that blemished his face, as well as a faint, rapidly healing bruise by his eye. Kilderan seemed to slightly seize up under his scrutiny. Rynn shifted his attention back to the window.

"They're waiting," Kilderan muttered, though his tone was laced with concern.

The ramp on the ship came down and Rynn gingerly followed Kilderan towards the group of waiting pirates. Rynn let his gaze drift across the motley assembly and felt anxiety rising in the pit of his stomach. As soon as they stepped off of what Rynn had begun to regard as the only safety at all in his life, the space pirates immediately surrounded them and began to escort them into the nearest building.

As they plodded across the loud metal floor that led through the building, Rynn took in the establishment: it was a very small but busy outpost, consisting of a few small alcoves—possibly lodgings—and a ship maintenance station—and the largest of all, the prison where the pirates likely housed their most difficult assets.

They reached the entrance and Rynn exchanged glances with Kilderan. Another group of men emerged from within and took over the escort as the pirates deserted them.

Inside, the hallway was dimly lit and narrow and dusty. A foreign smell wafted through the chilled air and filled Rynn's nose, causing him to grow uncomfortable. They marched down the hallway and entered a few doors, though to Rynn it all happened within heartbeats and in a perplexing blur.

They turned a corner and Rynn realized they had arrived at their destination. The jailers stepped forward.

"Your weapons," said one of them.

Kilderan slowly unbuckled the knife sheath and holster from his hip and the guard confiscated it. Rynn reluctantly handed over the dagger Asold had given him and Asold's staff.

And then they were directed into a cell, one of two infinitely long rows of ones exactly like it. Kilderan did not say nor do a thing, and Rynn seated himself on the thin cot against the wall as the previously dormant pain in his arm began to flare up. The guards deserted them and fell into an incomprehensible conversation, which lingered for a short while longer than they did before fading as well.

Kilderan seemed to relax slightly. His head then snapped up and he hurriedly paced over to Rynn. "Let me see your arm," he said softly.

Rynn held out the appendage and watched as Kilderan bent over it attentively, dark hair hanging over his face. The strip of fabric they had replaced Kilderan's mask with was now caked with a small amount of clotted blood, but when his hands loosened the makeshift bandage, Rynn saw that although it still stung, it had begun to heal and now the only fluid flowing from it was lymph.

"If the jailers notice how peculiar your blood looks they will undoubtedly become suspicious," Kilderan muttered, mostly to himself. He then unbuttoned and removed his long, black coat to reveal a soft tunic that fell loosely to his hips that was equally dark. He offered the jacket to Rynn. "Put this on. Use it to cover the wound." Rynn accepted the garb and thrust his arms into the sleeves that were far too long as Kilderan continued, "We cauterized the wound and stopped the bleeding back on the ship, but it could start bleeding again and we can't risk anyone noticing that."

"Notice what, exactly?" came a voice from somewhere outside their cell.

Kilderan stepped past Rynn and sidled up to the bars. He squinted.

Staying behind, Rynn attempted to fit the coat more snugly around his waist using its belt. However, he looked up when a man emerged from the shadow of the cell across from the one he and Kilderan were being detained in.

He appeared to be a man around a decade older than Kilderan, and he wore a stained white tunic and baggy tan breeches. His head was shaved, though his face bore an untidy red-blonde beard. "How do you do, gentlemen?" He smirked. "What are you in for?"

Kilderan did not reply, simply scrutinizing the man even more.

"I was kind of glad to have that cell emptied." He sighed. "The last guy was only in here for a day or two, but he was just so blasted annoying. Blathering on about some girl he needed to get back to or something like that." He leaned against the bars of his cell, relaxed.

Kilderan took a step back as Rynn joined him at his side and looked up at the young man's profile, at his furrowed brow and distant gaze. He murmured something that Rynn did not hear.

The strange man continued to rant about something likely inappropriate that Rynn did not care to listen to.

Kilderan's stupor was finally broken as his eyes widened. He then peered at the man. "Wait…Jack? Yojackson Owens?"

The man halted in his speech and, after several moments of gawking at Kilderan, also seemed to be filled with some sort of vague recognition. "…Kip? Kip, is that you?"

"Yes! Yes, it's me, Jack!" It was the most joy Rynn had ever seen his new companion exhibit.

Yojackson, as the man was called, smiled, a wide grin filled with perfect teeth, save one that was badly chipped. "Why, shoot, Kip, you turned out to be a pretty handsome son of a gun, though I doubt I could say the same for myself!" The criminal cackled.

"You underrate yourself, Jack." A smile almost broke across Kilderan's aloof and haunted features. Rynn beamed.

"How did you end up in here?" Kilderan asked. He glanced around at the hallway before adding, "I thought…I thought the emperor sentenced you to be hanged. What are you doing in a pirate hideout on a moon?"

"Yeah…They saved my hide a while back and apparently expected payment for it, which I obviously would not yield. But at least I'm not wearing that thrice blasted yellow suit this time." Yojackson suppressed a scoff and his eyes shone as he added, "And the sentence? They underestimated me." He shot a quick wink at Rynn, then returned his attention to Kilderan only to glance back at the boy. "And who are you?"

"Rynn. Rynn Hera, sir." Rynn immediately liked the criminal, despite just that, for anyone who was evidently so friendly with Kilderan he felt he ought to respect.

Yojackson scratched his chin and an array of rings flashed in the flickering lights. "Rynn Hera…" he began.

He cocked his head and exchanged a look with Kilderan, though Rynn did not at all comprehend what had passed between them.

"How did *you* end up in here?" Yojackson queried. "What are you even doing running around the galaxy with a child, Kip?"

Kilderan cast his gaze to the ground. "I'm not entirely sure. Are pirates common around here?"

Yojackson interrupted him with a scoff. "Have you *been* to Umeda?"

"What do you mean?"

"This crew's activity seems to have escalated recently. It has gotten worse. They've been coming down to the surface and plundering, too. They even plundered my ship!" He shrugged and shook his head.

Kilderan frowned.

Yojackson continued, "So who knows how long you two will be in here, huh? And like I asked before, what are you *really* doing anyway?"

Kilderan turned back to Rynn, lips pressed into a firm line. "I am trying to save him," he said gravely.

Rynn crept up to Kilderan's side and the taller man bent towards his lips. Rynn whispered, "What are the two of you talking about? Who is that man?"

Just as softly, Kilderan replied, "He and I have known each other since I was very young. He knows about your blood." Rynn's eyes widened with panic, prompting Kilderan to quickly add, "But we can trust him. Don't worry. He can probably help us."

"Help us do what? Kilderan—" But Yojackson had resumed his speech and Kilderan seemed engrossed.

"I *can* help you," Yojackson was saying, "But we need to get out of this blasted hole first."

Rynn stepped forward. "How are we supposed to do that?"

V

Rynn sat in a strangely fashioned starship made entirely of glass, his legs crossed and his hands folded in his lap. The stars and moons and suns and planets performed an intricate dance, seemingly for his entertainment. They swirled in and out of one another in an almost liquid manner. He felt a strange sensation inside his chest, a feeling of simultaneous assurance and emptiness.

A sharp pain stung his palms, then, and he glanced down.

His hands were covered in lustrous, pulsing blood. He cried out wordlessly and attempted to wipe the blood off on his pants, but it stained even his bones. A resounding thunder filled his ears. Looking out of the glass ship, he saw the three suns, prominent and scarlet red, the same shade as his blood. Every star in the sky glittered like some kind of ethereal confetti.

He felt hands grasp his shoulders and craned his neck to see Kilderan standing behind him. "You are the son of a goddess," he said.

Asold joined the perplexing assembly. "Rynn, listen to me. I know—"

Blood filled the starship and every corner of Rynn's consciousness and body.

"The forbidden son of a goddess and a mortal."

"The emperor will find you and do horrible, dreadful things to you."

"We have to leave."

The moon's orbit eventually caused the light of the suns to shine in through the window over Rynn and Kilderan's cell, an ethereal light that cast a ruddy glow all over the area and revealed that there was much more dust in the air than was visible previously.

Rynn opened his eyes and coughed. His eyes watered and he frowned as he tried to recall falling asleep. His body quivered suddenly. He rolled onto his side.

Kilderan had seated himself on the cot and its taut sheet. He stared at his folded hands and occasionally glanced up at Rynn, his eyes adopting an eerie luminescence, a fiery blue.

A curious flavor had settled in Rynn's mouth as he rose from the cot and the image of Yojackson's body against the cell bars began to burn itself into his vision as he awaited the criminal's supposedly promising plan.

There were a few moments of fleeting tranquility before one of their unsavory captors sauntered up to the cells.

Rynn watched as Yojackson murmured some strange oath, causing the pirate to turn.

"What?" the captor barked.

Yojackson spread his palms and said something in an undertone as Rynn turned to Kilderan.

"You are trying to save me? Why did you say that so seriously? Where are we really going?"

Kilderan looked up into Rynn's eyes. "...Away? I—I don't know. Anywhere but Arsteine. And I said I was going to protect you, didn't I? So I will. You must understand how important it is that we get your blood as far from Emperor Dusek as possible."

Rynn shifted. Any time Kilderan spoke of Arsteine's emperor, he spoke with a tone of traumatic petrification, and although it was so subtle it was nearly nonexistent, it caused a chill of dread to overtake Rynn. Something inside of him was glad Kilderan, who obviously knew the emperor's desperate dealings with the goddesses, did not elaborate on the "horrible things".

"Kilderan—" Rynn began.

They both tensed up as a loud clatter sounded outside the cell. Yojackson grabbed the collar of his shirt through the bars and bashed the man's head against the cell. Using his free hand, Yojackson also pounded the pirate's face a few times. He released his hold and the man slumped over after the criminal's fierce assault.

Rynn stared after Yojackson, and then asked, "Now what?"

Yojackson held up a pistol and raised his eyebrows. He aimed the gun at the small computer that managed the lock on his cell and shot it.

Yojackson's cell door opened and he stepped out with something akin to an air of victory. He approached the cell Rynn and Kilderan were being held in. "Stand back," he warned.

They complied and he fired at their cell as well.

The three of them immediately rushed down the hallway with a silent but hurried pace.

"If we have any luck at all, then my ship will be awaiting our departure outside," Yojackson informed them.

As they trotted through the corridor, Rynn began to glance around, puzzled that there were not more guards watching the pirates' only captives. But then he heard a gun click.

Yojackson halted and the three of them stared at the pirate standing before them. He fumbled with his holster, but Yojackson shot him as soon as the pirate's gloved finger curled around the trigger.

They approached his now-limp body and Kilderan stooped to retrieve the handgun, which he nestled into his own holster.

They proceeded.

They emerged a few moments later into the large hangar they had landed in when the pirates had taken them into custody.

"There!" Yojackson pointed.

Rynn and Kilderan turned to the direction his gesture indicated. Before them sat a huge cargo hauling ship that appeared to be battered from a battle, gleaming beneath the hangar lights.

"Let's get out of here, then," Kilderan said.

"But what about your ship?" Rynn asked.

There was a chorus of shouts and a series of heavy thuds on the floor of the shabby, abandoned station.

Kilderan turned to Rynn and Yojackson. "Forget the ship. I just need to get Rynn out of here."

Rynn bit back the words that immediately sprang to his lips. *They have my grandfather's staff. That's all I have left of him.* He glanced up at Kilderan, but the man was not looking at him.

They scrambled for Yojackson's ship just as a score of pirates flooded into the hangar.

"Hurry!" the criminal yelled as Rynn and Kilderan skirted him.

Rynn's ears filled with the thunder of firing guns and the trio immediately ducked behind one of the pirates' small fighter ships as bullets ricocheted off its hull.

Yojackson stood and fired a few times after steadying his aim. "Head for the ship!"

Rynn glanced back at the advancing pirates at the same time Kilderan was pulling the ship's ramp down with a loud crash.

Then he turned to Yojackson, who had his gun aimed and was awaiting the pirates to weave their way around the other ships stored in the hangar. A shot fired.

Kilderan guided Rynn into the sizable cargo hauler and Yojackson made for the cockpit.

The ship had been in a minor state of disrepair on its exterior, and while it was much larger than Kilderan's fighter, it was even more run-down inside: crates and a few sloppily folded blankets were littered about the main area; parts of both the exterior and interior had been mended with differing metals so the ship appeared like some burnished iron patchwork quilt; the cockpit was isolated from the passenger area, with a door separating them.

Yojackson shoved the clutter aside as he hurried to the pilot's seat.

Kilderan did not sit, and Rynn mirrored him in gripping a part of the ship as it took off, albeit in a rickety manner.

"They just refueled her! Looks like they thought they were gonna keep her!" Yojackson called from the inside the cockpit.

Yojackson then aimed for the hangar control panel against the wall and fired at it, causing the huge hangar doors to open.

"You can't just shoot everything to solve your problems, Jack!" Kilderan called.

"It worked, didn't it?" came the smug reply.

The ship picked up its pace and they unsteadily maneuvered out of the pirates' makeshift hideaway.

There was a sudden impact accompanied by a thud as Rynn moved to take his seat. He looked to the cockpit.

"Sorry!" Yojackson yelled through the cockpit's open door. "Someone put a wall there!"

Soon they had broken free into wide, open nothingness and Rynn felt the ship lurch beneath him as it sped frantically away from the abandoned outpost. The entire skeleton of the ship rumbled as it cruised through space and Umeda began to shrink and disappear behind them.

Finally, Kilderan joined Rynn on the hard bench after clearing away a small handgun. "At least they didn't loot the ship," he muttered.

Rynn sat forward. "They took my staff."

Kilderan faced him.

"It was my grandfather's. It was the only thing I had of his." He folded his hands and tapped his foot against the bench.

"I'm sorry," Kilderan said. He paused before adding, "But who knows how long we would have been in there if they had captured us a second time. And I'm trying—"

"—to protect me," Rynn interrupted, "I know. But what does that even involve?"

"Yeah, Kip, what is your plan for us now, anyway?" Yojackson joined in.

Rynn gazed up at Kilderan as he proceeded to ponder his comrades' questions.

After several moments of anticipation, he finally responded. "I am going to return Rynn to the stars." With that ambiguous statement, he turned to Rynn. "If you remain in our world, the world of the mortals, Emperor Dusek will find you."

"What are you suggesting, Kip?" Yojackson was skeptical.

"There is a spring, somewhere in this galaxy…" He inhaled. "That's where I have to take Rynn if I want him to be safe. If he goes into the celestial spring, he'll be in the sky, he'll no longer be part of this world. He'll be safe."

"The celestial spring? How do even know it really exists?" Yojackson protested.

Rynn did not realize his lips were parted until his mouth had grown dry. He wet his lips and then asked Kilderan, "What would happen to me?"

"You would no longer be like us, like mortals. The blood makes you immortal, like the goddesses, and so you can join them. We can save you, Rynn. We can make sure the emperor never lays a hand on you."

Rynn frowned and he averted his gaze, eyes glistening. *I would join the goddesses, my mother… I would leave this world.* He was young and could not comprehend every consequence and complication, but he trusted Kilderan.

Yojackson leaned back in the pilot's seat. "How are you so sure that's even an option? And I think you should let Rynn decide if he even wants to go with a bunch of high and mighty strangers to who knows where!"

"It isn't anyone's choice!" Kilderan said, his voice rising. "It's what I have to do if Rynn is to be kept safe! You of all people should understand what I need to do, Yojackson!" Reckless desperation saturated his voice.

Rynn had fallen silent amidst the arguing adults, and the overwhelming thoughts surged in his mind.

The ship lurched, shifting the crates and blankets. Rynn's knees knocked against one another. A lock of his hair fell into his face. The voices of Kilderan and Yojackson became a suppressed, muffled droning.

The voices became distinguishable again.

"I just think that it's a pretty vague idea, and a bloody hasty one," Yojackson stated, his voice slightly calmer now.

Kilderan's shoulders relaxed as he glanced at Rynn and then stared at the back of Yojackson's head. "Well, maybe—"

Something inside the cockpit began to beep and Rynn sat up and pointed. "What's that sound?"

Kilderan shifted closer to Rynn, a hand darting up to his neck, and followed the direction of Rynn's finger.

Yojackson forsook his relaxed position and punched a command into the control area. "Hey, Kip…Someone's hailing us. They called you a—"

Kilderan leapt from his seat. "Get us out of here now! Go, Jack, go *now*!" He rushed to the cockpit and into the copilot's seat.

Rynn stood and ambled up to the doorway of the cockpit. "What's happening? Who are those ships?"

"Get us to anywhere but here!" Kilderan yelled. Fear completely overtook his face and tone as he whispered, "They've found me."

VI

Rynn had not believed it was possible for the cargo ship that barely flew straight to go even faster than it already was, but Yojackson managed to create a distance between the unseen ship and their own careening vessel.

Rynn stood and joined Kilderan in the cockpit, but as he was about to question the meaning of their escape, he noticed the blatant fear across Kilderan's features. He stared out of the window towards an asteroid belt that they were quickly approaching.

Yojackson steered the ship so that it was on its side and though his agility was far from excellent he succeeded in dodging every one of the cold, dismal rocks that drifted around lifelessly and likely watched the satellites capable of movement with no small degree of envy.

The sky before them was of a deep, otherworldly blue that blurred as soon as the ship began its jump.

Rynn saw Kilderan relax slightly, though his eyes seemed to burn with the nameless emotion.

They appeared before another empty sky when the ship finally slowed, and Rynn stepped back. "Who was in that ship?"

Yojackson glanced at Kilderan, who said nothing, though it was clear that a thousand complex thoughts whirred through his mind.

"It doesn't matter," he finally said. "Find the nearest spaceport and we can dock there."

Yojackson moved to comply, but then halted. "Blast. They're back."

Kilderan immediately stiffened again.

The ship shook suddenly.

"They've fired at us!" Yojackson exclaimed. "What should we do?"

Kilderan turned to Rynn. "Rynn, get in the back of the ship. Jack, we're going to have to fight them...Do we have a chance of destroying them?"

Yojackson smirked. "Do you *know* who you're flying with?" He spun the ship around and then said, "I've scanned them. It's a very small fighter, so we can likely destroy them."

Rynn had begun to obey Kilderan when he caught sight of the vessel Yojackson had just described. It was small, sleek, and black—much like Kilderan's ship. But then he squinted at it when he noticed a symbol on its side. It was a familiar symbol: the same emblem that had been embroidered onto the flag of the boys at the festival.

Emperor Dusek's insignia. But why would Kilderan be—

The ship rumbled as it let loose a blast upon the smaller fighter, causing its wing to fly off and into a burning orbit around the vessel it had been amputated from.

Rynn had finally taken cover amongst the cargo in the rear of the ship, reminding him of when he had fled from his grandfather's killers and hid in the closet. His breathing was rapid, though he did not notice. His eyes were on Kilderan, who looked as if every demon outside of the world of flesh and blood was about to be released upon the cargo ship and its alarmed crew.

Yojackson fired upon the craft in succession, and finally after evading the blasts it succumbed to his determination and exploded in a brilliant display of sparks and scorched metal.

"Blast it," Yojackson muttered. "They didn't hit us very hard, but they hit us a lot, and according to the status indicator our engine is in danger."

Kilderan, releasing the copilot's controls and gripping the arm of his seat, released a pent-up breath. "Can we reach the closest spaceport?"

Yojackson fiddled with the ship's map and then replied, "Just barely."

"Get us there," Kilderan breathed. He then deserted the copilot's seat and sought out Rynn.

The boy gazed up at him and took the hand that was offered to him. "Who were they?"

Kilderan shifted and scanned his own body, as if he now felt wary in his own skin. Releasing Rynn's hand slowly, he said, "They were the emperor's men, sort of like the ones who killed your grandfather."

The ship lurched, leaping once again across the stars.

Rynn's eyes widened. "How did they find us all the way out here?"

Kilderan shook his head. He turned and gazed out of the cockpit window for a long while before seating himself on the bench and gesturing for Rynn to do the same, eyes alight with emotion.

Rynn joined him, toying with the edge of a blanket as he did.

"We're lucky that they were only flying a small fighter ship." He sighed.

"But…Yojackson said they called you something?" Rynn squinted at Kilderan. "What's going on?"

He watched as the young man's eyes wandered to the cockpit window, visible through the open door. He mirrored Kilderan's posture and sat silently as he stared out the ship's window at the speeding stars, his eyelashes creating a brilliant, variegated nimbus around his vision as the light shone through them.

The sound of Kilderan's voice startled him. "There is something that I need to tell you, Rynn." His face seemed pained, and yet also hopeful.

Rynn's brow creased. The weight of Kilderan's tone set him on edge. "What—what is it?"

"I think—"

"We've made it," Yojackson announced. "I'll find us a place to land." A series of clicks followed.

The spaceport was a long, wide outpost containing numerous hangars and a large entrance to its interior. Neon advertisements and flashing lights greeted their landing ship.

"Port Illuvar," Yojackson said. "We're lucky that this was the nearest outpost." He looked back at Rynn. "It's kind of the halfway point for most interstellar travels. They have a marketplace, and a tavern, and a few shops. We can get more weapons," he explained.

"But, we can't land in that hangar or hail them, because they'll likely recognize my identification. We'll have to enter from outside of the buildings with airlock." Yojackson then stood and made his way towards one of the many compartments in the cargo ship and began to rummage through it. He soon emerged with a bundle of unusual looking fabric, saying, "There isn't any oxygen out there, at least not until we make it into the port." He tossed the fabric, which Rynn discovered to actually be some kind of outlandish suit, to them and ordered for them to equip it. "It's a little awkward to wear at first, because it's a really outdated design, but it comes in handy."

Kilderan examined the garment. "How do you have these?"

Yojackson gestured with a jab of his thumb to the closet behind him. "There are a few more in there. They were likely used by the previous crew."

Rynn turned to the criminal. "Previous crew? Did you steal this ship?"

Yojackson quickly smothered the glint in his eye that seemed like something akin to pride. "I was in a bind. I had to make some quick decisions."

Rynn only half believed him. He examined the cumbersome suit and its strange mask before trying to slip into the arm and leg holes. Once he was in the suit, he attempted to swing his arms and become more comfortable.

Rynn then glanced at Kilderan, who was donning the slightly baggy spacesuit himself. As he thrust his arms into the sleeves, the sleeves of his own black tunic slid back.

Rynn studied his arms and the bruises they bore, as well as a bandage bound slightly above one wrist in what seemed like a hurried manner.

Kilderan quickly lowered the sleeves, although Rynn doubted the young man had noticed he had been watching.

Yojackson then approached them with a poorly mended rucksack in one clenched fist. "The pirates looted me, but I'm not so ignorant that I wouldn't stash a little something in a more secretive place." He reached for his boot to tap it fondly and then gestured at the rucksack. "There are a few credits in here, for if we need it."

They disembarked Yojackson's ship after docking at the spacious landing bay and started towards the huge metal sanctuary, and Rynn glanced back at the ship as his feet fell in unison with Kilderan's upon the metal floor. Yojackson sauntered up to the portal to the spaceport and the doors automatically opened to make way for their entrance.

To Rynn, it was almost completely different inside: they had left behind the cold, imposing metal edifice, and were now faced with what seemed like a long, wide, bronze-colored hall, with booths on either side and entrances to metal grottos inset into the walls that acted as venues for more permanent businesses.

It was like a condensed city, as if someone had attempted to fit the essence of sprawling Thruhairth into one cramped spaceport, with the visitors carrying their bundles of purchased goods and the merchants calling out advertisements for their products with the aid of flashing, vibrant holograms. The grimy metal floor was littered with discarded papers and wrappings and a few bolts. The light of the suns streamed in and bathed the entire space in a cheerful golden light almost too jaunty for the fact that the outpost was floating in the darkness of space and not located on a planet.

Countless colorful banners were hung from the ceiling, their most prominent flags those that bore the emblem of every lord and lady presiding over each planet in the galaxy. Rynn followed Kilderan's eyes to the soft blue banner with Emperor Dusek's insignia.

But then Kilderan turned and the three of them removed their masks and began to wade through the diverse crowd that occupied the sky-born outpost.

Yojackson's gaze passed between every neon sign indicating a tavern or restaurant. Rynn found it difficult to keep from doing the same, for every cart they passed bore tantalizing aromas and the hiss of vendors frying food. He once glimpsed a chef turning an odd-looking amphibious creature on a spit.

A group of strange but elegantly dressed women strolled past, blinking their long eyelashes and parting their unusually colored lips. One of them smiled at Rynn.

They exchanged glances with one another and every one of them could tell what the others were pondering: Where to visit first?

As if answering the much-contemplated question, Yojackson moved to stand in front of Rynn and Kilderan and held up his hands, saying, "We need to find a mechanic. The ship's in pretty bad shape."

Kilderan nodded and the two of them vanished, merging with the crowd and leaving Rynn to be swept by the whirlwind of armor and silk and baggage and trader carts. He glanced around, looking for the shaved head and earrings, or for the tousled brown hair, but to no avail. He took a few anxious steps forward and then tried calling out. "Yojackson! Kilderan! Hey!"

No reply.

He shoved through the crowd and past the booths, evading a little girl and her mother as he sped up slightly. He collided with a bulky man in a soiled tunic, who frowned at Rynn and then muttered something unintelligible as he stepped away.

"Kilderan! Kilderan! Yojackson! Where are you?"

He nearly ran into a second man, but this one was a merchant with greasy black hair and a light purple jacket wearing queer goggles who spun around before Rynn could plow into him. In one hand he stabilized a wheeled rack displaying a multitude of pairs of the same goggles he wore. "You look like you need some of these, son!" he said jovially.

"Um, no thank you," Rynn said hurriedly as he broke into a run and continued to call out Yojackson and Kilderan's names. He was beginning to grow distressed and he passed through a region of the spaceport where he wished he still had Asold's staff.

The area had almost no merchant booths or carts and was shaded by a canopy that turned the rays of the suns an unnatural amalgam of scarlet and indigo. Neon signs flickered and Rynn heard a giggle as a man pursued an aquatic-looking alien woman in the entrance of one of the darkened hollows like those the three travelers had seen earlier.

A few pairs of eyes followed the boy as he left the area and continued to bound throughout the station. "Kilderan! Yojackson! Kil—" He ran right into someone again, and his cries were smothered.

He backed up and lifted his gaze. He gave a relieved sigh as he saw Kilderan's blue eyes and Yojackson's bearded face staring back at him. Kilderan, too, seemed to sigh gratefully.

"Where have you been, Jynn? We've been looking all over for you and Kip has been so worried," Yojackson said, clapping a hand to Rynn's shoulder.

"It's Rynn, not Jynn," Rynn said.

Kilderan bent to level himself with Rynn. "Are you okay? We didn't realize you fell behind until I turned and you weren't there…"

"I'm all right."

43

Kilderan held out his hand and Rynn took it gingerly, suddenly remembering the bruises and scars on the man's arms, though he very much wanted to forget.

"Don't let go, okay?" Kilderan said.

He said it so seriously Rynn was caught unaware for a heartbeat. "I—I won't."

Kilderan resumed his full height and as they began walking Yojackson said, "All right. I asked about a mechanic, and I was told there would be one just up ahead."

They continued through the spaceport, following closely behind Yojackson.

Kilderan towed Rynn along by the hand and several patrons of various merchants stared after the trio of an escaped criminal, a mysterious savior, and a severely important child, though Rynn was certain none of the few onlookers who bothered to scrutinize them had any idea who they really were, who *he* really was.

It made him feel as if he had some advantage over everyone else, with the knowledge that the celestial ichor ran through his veins and allowed him immortal life, if he had understood Kilderan's comments earlier.

Rynn, Kilderan, and Yojackson came upon a portal in the wall of the spaceport, and Kilderan slowly released his grip on Rynn's hand.

Yojackson stopped short. "Here it is, if the information was accurate. Supposedly the guy in here will fix our ship up for a very affordable price." He held up the rucksack that held the hidden coins he had stashed.

The ship mechanic's shop was dimly lit compared to the main district of Port Illuvar, and Rynn's feet landed on a metal grate on the floor when they stepped down into the dusty shop.

Rynn let his gaze wander around the shabby space. Shelves with crudely organized stockpiles of tools such as welding irons and wrenches, tubs of miscellaneous computer chips, and a tub of stained rags were backed against the wall nearest Rynn and his companions. A small metal table holding a strange little robotic machine filled the furthest corner.

The clinking of hundreds of minuscule nuts and bolts startled him and he found himself staring at a husky, almost reptilian man who wore coveralls that through the medium of faded oil stains and loose, frayed threads told the story of his labor.

"Can I help you?" he asked in a raspy voice.

"Yes," Yojackson said. "I have a ship in need of repairs. We were in a, uh, bit of a tussle before we were able to make it here." He attempted that confident smirk.

The man burst into a hearty chuckle. "Ah, I see. I get those kinds of customers all the time!" He turned and snatched a small device from one of the carts behind him and neared Yojackson. "What hangar is your ship located in and what model?"

Yojackson's gaze darted to the ceiling. "Eh…No hangar. But it's an Aristarchus, exploration and cargo."

The man nodded knowingly and, trying to suppress another bout of genial laughter, handed Yojackson a small microchip. "Don't lose that, it's the only way I keep track of my customers." Another ebullient laugh.

Yojackson took the chip and stuffed it into the pocket of his spacesuit. He thanked and then saluted the man as he led Rynn and Kilderan out of the shop and back into the open carnival of flashing holograms and rippling flags.

"Now what?" Rynn asked, gazing around at the crowd that had dissipated slightly because of the meal hour.

"Now we eat," Yojackson said. "I spotted a fine-looking tavern a while back."

"Lead the way," Kilderan said, glancing over his shoulder at Rynn, who followed closely behind.

VII

A tall glass filled to its brim with a bizarre ultramarine liquid and topped with ice cubes slid across the table to Yojackson's ready hands. The uninterested barmaid then passed a lemon-yellow drink in a shorter glass to Kilderan. She did not even glance at Rynn.

Rynn watched Yojackson quaff the beverage and then shifted his attention to Kilderan, who had barely touched his drink. He was about to say something to Kilderan when the waitress returned with a startlingly green drink in a tall, slender beaker and handed it to Rynn.

"Uh…We didn't order that," Kilderan told her.

"The bartender wants him to try it. Says he'll like it." She seemed to stifle a chuckle as she left them.

Rynn stared down into the liquid and Yojackson leaned in as he did.

"Go ahead," Yojackson urged.

Rynn used both hands to lift the glass and brought it to his lips. He winced as the bitter taste bit his tongue. It left a faint burning sensation after rushing down his throat.

Disgusted, he began to cough and his eyes watered as he spat out the remainder of the drink.

Yojackson cringed at him and he waited for the fit to subside before lifting the flute again. Kilderan took his hand and shoved it and the drink back onto the table.

"Are you all right?" Kilderan asked with a brief glare in Yojackson's direction.

Rynn blinked a few times and then nodded before wiping beads of the liquid from his chin. "What *was* that?"

"Some kind of really strong liquor," Yojackson answered, and then to Kilderan he exclaimed, "What is that look for, Kip?"

"You told him to drink it!"

Yojackson opened his mouth and then clamped it shut again, leaning back against his cushioned seat. A few seconds passed before he asked, "Shall we order our food?"

•••

The tavern Yojackson had brought them to was not one filled with winking fluorescents and performers dressed in glittering robes and tables occupied with dignitaries, like those they had passed on their route, but rather one hosting armored bounty hunters and merchants on their breaks. There was a small band in the back corner and one singer who, despite her environment, was dressed rather elegantly.

Kilderan constantly scanned the area and occasionally glanced at Rynn's healed arm.

The waitress, returned for the third time, brought with her a tray of curious dishes that she set on the table before them: a bowl of maroon paste heavy with herbs and that bubbled slightly, a plate of leaves that acted as a bed for some unfortunate, wrinkled, pink, curled-up creature, and a small saucer of fried teal tubers. Rynn's eyes widened and he glanced at both Kilderan and Yojackson.

They said nothing, and so Rynn, too, was hushed as he tasted small portions of the meal. He was surprised to find it palatable, with the rat-like animal being the most savory.

He paused eating and stared at a woman sitting in a corner with her head downcast, fiddling with something in her hands below the table. But then her head snapped up and she slowly stood and made her way over to the bar counter.

"So," Yojackson began in a whisper after dropping his chopsticks onto the plate with a chink, "Where are we going after this?"

Rynn gave him a confused look.

"Where is this spring you told us about? What's your plan, Kip?"

Rynn's stomach clenched.

Kilderan shot a perturbed glance at the tavern's exit before he leaned in. "Supposedly there is some place out there where we can find the spring, some comet or—or moon, or..." He clenched his jaw slightly. "It exists. That's how the goddesses were able to assume their mortal forms and live amongst us."

Rynn followed Kilderan's glance, but his once again landed on the pink-haired woman at the counter, who now had a drink even taller than Yojackson's in her hands. She glanced over her shoulder in his direction and he averted his gaze, returning to his own business.

Yojackson frowned. "Doesn't that seem a bit far-fetched to you?"

Kilderan's lips were a firm line. "I know it's out there somewhere." He turned and, with tenderness in his eyes, said to Rynn, "You will come with me, won't you? You will let me save you?"

It had never been more evident to Rynn that Kilderan was withholding something from him, for the yearning in his normally reserved tone was so intense that it threatened to make Rynn squirm in his seat. "But how do you know it will work?"

"The spring will know you carry the celestial blood. You can simply wade in the pool and shed your flesh for light."

The prospect frightened Rynn. He did not want to leave behind the world he had only just begun to grow acquainted with.

Kilderan saw the concern in his eyes, and as if reading his thoughts said, "I just need you to trust me, trust what I say. There is a marvelous, wonderful world amongst the heavens that was meant for you. Not here. Not so long as people like the emperor are so desperate that they will do anything to get ahold of the celestial blood."

"I trust you. I know it's dangerous." Rynn looked into his eyes, which dilated. "And it scares me every day, every time I think about it. You know what I need to do, and I…I think you should do it." His words seemed to release Kilderan, if only a little, from the strange shell of apprehension that coated his mind and his movements.

"Come on," Kilderan said, shifting. "The ship might be ready by now."

The three of them stood in unison and left the tavern, and when Rynn glanced back, the woman was gone.

• • •

Afterwards they wandered rather aimlessly around the spaceport, simply eyeing every booth and cart they passed as they retraced their route to Port Illuvar's entrance.

They walked for a few more moments before Yojackson halted. Looking back, he said, "I believe I am in need of a new jacket."

Rynn and Kilderan followed him to a rickety-looking cart sitting amongst racks of tunics and robes and jackets and trousers for sale, though the clothing looked dusty and threadbare. Rynn frowned, but then remembered Yojackson's supply of money, though it was limited.

The pirate began to rifle through the racks and then Rynn almost jumped as he heard a loud "Ah!"

Turning, he saw Yojackson hold up a maroon jacket for inspection.

Rynn thought of his own tattered, dusty, bloodied clothes and then looked at Kilderan. "I don't think there's anything here that could fit me."

Kilderan tore his gaze from the boy and his wide eyes and examined a few of the racks before staring up at an ivory tunic that was hanging on the cart. He reached for it, completely ignored by the clerk who stared at a flickering hologram consisting of intensely bright, fast, flashing scenes.

"What about this?"

Rynn took the tunic and held it against his body. It fell slightly past his thighs, but not quite to his knees. "It might work." He walked over to Yojackson and laid the tunic over the jacket as the clerk absently scanned the clothes and then took Yojackson's money.

"Let's get out of here," Yojackson said when he had the bundle in his arms, which he stuffed in his rucksack. He looked at Kilderan. "There are probably some weapons in the *Aristarchus*' storage compartments that we can use." With a brief glance at Rynn, he said, "If you wanna protect this kid, I'd say we should start as soon as we can."

Rynn sidled up to Kilderan and, rather subconsciously, slipped his hand into Kilderan's. They exchanged a glance and then proceeded walking.

The massive spaceport's exit was in sight when Rynn heard someone call out to them.

"Wait!"

They all turned.

Rynn furrowed his brow. The voice belonged to the strange woman with the rose-colored locks from the tavern. She wore a brown leather jacket and black breeches, though her ornate earrings and necklace seemed unfitting for the rest of her outfit.

Yojackson glanced around. "Uh…Who are you?"

The woman did not answer him, instead saying to Rynn in a low voice, "I know what you are."

"What?" He stepped away, his back against Kilderan. The latter tensed up.

"I heard you and your companions talking about the celestial spring."

Yojackson stiffened. "…What spring?"

The woman's lips tightened. "I know he carries the blood of the goddesses. I know you three are trying to locate the spring." She studied Rynn for a moment, before moving to examine the two men. "I know someone who knows where it is. Well, where it should be."

Kilderan's lips parted and he eyed her with hesitation. "How do you know this?"

She cocked her head thoughtfully. "There are a lot of things I am not going to tell you. But that is something you will have to accept if you want my help."

"She could be lying," Yojackson muttered to Kilderan.

"Or she isn't." His blue eyes flashed at Rynn. "Somehow she knew about him." To the stranger, he asked, "Why would you help us?"

"I am a celestial priestess," she explained, partially uncurling her palm to reveal a string of queer-looking beads and charms, "so I have helped a lot of people. And I know a lot of things. And he's only a child. We can't allow him to fall into the wrong hands." She again focused on Rynn.

Kilderan was rigid behind Rynn, and his breath came in a slow but odd rhythm. "We'll let you come with us." To Yojackson, he added, "Anyone who has any notions like that, real or not, can't be allowed to just wander around the galaxy."

"What if she's one of those assassins that chased us all those days ago?" Rynn asked.

"She isn't," Kilderan replied. "I've seen beads like those before. What she says about being a priestess is true. If she was an assassin, you would already be far, far away from here."

Rynn frowned.

"All right," Yojackson said in a louder voice, "You'll come with us then."

The woman came nearer to them and politely bowed to Kilderan, who flinched before repeating the gesture. "My name is Aome Yusef."

Kilderan swallowed. "I'm Kilderan Quan."

"Yojackson Owens." The name's owner smirked.

Aome looked down at Rynn as the boy said, "My name is Rynn Hera."

• • •

"So…Who is this person who knows about the spring?" Kilderan asked from the copilot's seat when they were back on the ship. "I didn't realize it was such common knowledge."

"It isn't," Aome said. "The one I am taking you to knows many things for certain that all other mortals assume to be myth or rumor."

The ship's body hummed as Yojackson initiated its jump into space, leaving Port Illuvar to become a fading blur on the horizon.

Rynn had begun to analyze Aome even more now that he sat mere inches from her. Her skin was pale, but adorning it were even paler opalescent markings around her eyes, forehead, and cheeks that were visible only when the light illuminated her face, and even then just faintly. Her eyes were a muted shade of emerald and her hair was the color of blushing pink roses. Her soft features did not suit her bold demeanor or her worn clothing.

Kilderan had grown distant and was staring into space. Rynn adjusted his new white tunic so that its sleeves did not swallow his arms whole, as they attempted to.

"Where, exactly, is this person located?" Yojackson asked, his tone laced with incredulity.

Aome listed her head and answered, "The temple of Kazari on Arsteine."

Kilderan's head jerked up and he twisted in his seat to face Aome. "We can't go to Arsteine. That's where we fled from."

Aome blinked at him. "And you will have to return if you want to really save Rynn."

"You don't understand. The emperor—"

"The emperor will find him if you don't listen to me and let us speak with the high priestess Velle Deka on Arsteine." Aome's slightly pointed eyebrows were furrowed and made a strange visor over her green eyes.

Kilderan shook his head and then looked at Rynn. Rynn stared back. Kilderan's eyes were filled with desperation, but Rynn's were filled with admiration: this friend of his, who had been a mere stranger just days ago, was so intent on protecting him and keeping Rynn's precious blood from those who would relish in harming him. He attempted a smile at Kilderan and immediately the young man softened.

"Yojackson, are we in a good place to just drift for a while?" Kilderan asked.

The rumbling of the ship ceased, dwindling into a subtle hum. "Yes."

"Try to get some sleep. We can talk more about this later, Aome." Kilderan stood and left the cockpit, retrieving a stack of the blankets Yojackson had once set atop the crates.

Rynn, wishing that the ship's only purpose was not cargo hauling and containment, watched as he spread them on the floor of the ship and then sat after tossing a bundle to Aome and Yojackson, also, as the criminal emerged from the cockpit. Rynn left his seat and settled next to Kilderan in his own makeshift bed, the hard floor only slightly softened by the stiff blankets that were not used to being unfolded. The ship gave one last grumble of protest before she, too, surrendered to the oblivious, ever-tranquil state of slumber.

VIII

Something was tugging at Rynn's consciousness when he awoke. His veins—for the first time in a long while—were quivering beneath his pale flesh, and the veins on his hands were bloated and in the light of whatever stray moons drifted near the ship he could see the veins of his arms, blue tendrils that if he stared hard enough he believed he could see the tremors that wracked them. His face was flushed and his throat dry. A small sigh sent a pang of alarm straight into his chest.

Looking over, he noticed the silhouette of Kilderan. The young man was sitting up, with his hands in his hair, his arms resting on his knees, and his face downcast. Another soft exhalation escaped him. There was a sniffling that Rynn almost did not hear.

Rynn's lips parted, but he did not make a sound, for he was uncertain of if he should say something.

The sleeves of Kilderan's tunic were rolled to his elbows and the strings that tied the neckline shut were unlaced, revealing a white scar on his sternum. He continued to breathe in a steady pattern, as if trying to comfort himself.

Rynn shifted in his bedding and Kilderan turned to face him. "Rynn..."

Rynn frowned. "Are you all right?"

Kilderan stared at the floor. "I couldn't sleep. I was just...thinking."

"About what?"

Kilderan finally met Rynn's gaze and he seemed distressed. "About what Aome proposed. I can't take you back to Arsteine. The only thing I had to do to keep you safe was to leave, and...and now she wants me to bring you back there."

Rynn pursed his lips. It was his turn to gaze into the bottom of the ship. "But..." He toyed with his sleeve. "If the priestess knows where the spring is, then we would have to return. If that's the only chance we've got to..." He fell silent as Kilderan buried his fingers deeper into his long, dark hair.

"I would never risk the chance of Emperor Dusek getting hold of you. I want to find the spring so you can live forever without fear or worry, and those are the only things that you will feel if the emperor finds you."

"I trust you, Kilderan. I know you will save me." Rynn's words served only to make Kilderan quieter and more somber. "And I know I don't have any idea what will happen if the emperor comes for me. If...If you feel like we shouldn't go back to Arsteine, I will follow you somewhere else."

Kilderan tore his hands from his hair and gingerly gripped one of Rynn's shoulders. "I would rather take you anywhere else, but I am afraid it's the only option. Anything else would be far too difficult, if I even had any other idea. I feel like Aome is telling the truth and that she can truly help us. It would be worse not to even speak with Velle Deka."

A light fell on Kilderan's face and illuminated his striking blue eyes so they smoldered with desperation, and it was then that Rynn noticed they were flooded with glistening tears. He averted his gaze and looked to the cockpit, where a shower of stars was falling peacefully. The dazzling show, Rynn knew, was tranquil and assuring from where he sat, but in actuality it was a deadly race that pitted the fiery comets against each other, one that not all would survive. He thought of his blood, the image of the glittering plasma flaring up inside his mind.

Rynn tapped his finger against his knee. "You're gonna let me go to Arsteine?"

Kilderan nodded, one soft, slow movement. Then he sighed again, almost a groan, and wove his hands through his hair once more. "I can't let the emperor get to you. I can't let him have your blood. The things he would do to you...I've seen it before, Rynn, I've—"

"You have been worried about saving me, but you're already doing that. How many times am I going to have to tell you I trust you and I believe in you?" Rynn's eyes grew wet. "If what you say about my blood being so highly coveted is true, then you're the only real friend I have. I don't know why you're crying." He grimaced.

"Because I know what will happen if I fail." His voice was low and monotone so as to not seem choked and faint.

I still don't understand why you care so much. I suppose I do: you know the value of the blood and I am only a child and the emperor is cruel.

"Don't cry, Rynn."

"But you're crying."

"I know." He edged towards Rynn and embraced him, then louder he said again, "I know."

• • •

The ship was not any more or less illumined with the passing of what its crew deemed night and the arrival of what they believed to be day. The only cause for Rynn's awakening was the rustling of everyone else's blankets and the sound of heavy boots on the floor right next to his ear.

He rolled onto his side and then hoisted himself up, taking with him the coarse blanket, which he balled up and placed with all of the others. Glancing around as he brought a hand up to smooth his hair, he noticed Yojackson adjusting his new jacket and Aome rousing the ship from its idleness. Kilderan sat behind him.

Everyone turned to Kilderan, whose long hair was ruffled and his eyelashes damp, as he ordered in a clear voice, "Take us to Arsteine."

Aome spun around. "Rynn will be safe. You'll see."

Kilderan said nothing and set to lacing up the strings of his tunic. Rynn let his gaze fall to Kilderan's boots before he positioned himself next to the man.

"If it's any consolation, I'm not too keen on heading for the capital planet myself," Yojackson began, scratching his head. "Not only am I concerned about the well-being of the kid, but you could say I'm quite a familiar face around there." A brief laugh escaped him. "It was my experiences on Arsteine that turned me into who I am now," he added, but did not elaborate.

"Arsteine is on the other end of the galaxy," Aome informed them. "Port Illuvar was a halfway point between Arsteine and its closest subordinate planets, but we jumped away from it in the opposite direction and we're now closest to Ganymede. That

55

mechanic fixed this ship up pretty good, and refueled it too, but he didn't touch the jump drive."

Yojackson sat forward. "What's wrong with the jump drive?"

"It's a bit burnt out. We can't make a single jump to Arsteine, and even if we did, this drive isn't exactly fast, so it would take weeks to enter the domain of the planets instead of mere empty space."

"Weeks?" Yojackson exclaimed. Mostly to himself, he muttered, "What kind of ship did I steal?"

"What are you suggesting?" Kilderan asked.

"According to the ship's estimate, it'll take longer to get back than it did to leap all the way out here, somehow. We'd have to make multiple stops at spaceports along the way, which costs money and time—"

"—which we don't have," Yojackson interjected.

"And…" Aome continued.

"…and you want to find a better jump drive." Kilderan finished.

Aome nodded. "The sooner we meet with Velle Deka, the sooner we find the spring you're so desperate to reach. I wouldn't call it a waste of time to hunt down a drive."

Kilderan sat back and thought, his eyes scanning Rynn. "And you think there's a chance some city on Ganymede will have one?"

Aome nodded again.

"Let's not waste any more time, then."

• • •

Although Ganymede was the closest planet to their location, they spent a series of jumps reaching it.

So far during the trek, none of them spoke. Rynn was only partially unsettled by the silence because he knew it was only born because all three of the adults were thinking. He, too, delved into the ponderation he guessed they were all partaking in: he, if all went according to Kilderan's plan, would soon leave the realm of mortal flesh and blood and fear and walk as a star amongst his mother and aunts, forever.

The prospect almost frightened him, for his mind became twisted and baffled whenever he considered the idea of time stretching on eternally, without an end, with himself and the goddesses the audience of whatever annihilation the mortals were doomed for. He would merely watch, and not participate, but he was filled with some innocent, childish sorrow of the mature realization that he would also never join in the cheer and mirth that mortals would.

He glanced down at his palms, like he had in the middle of the night, and stifled a sigh halfway through exhaling it. He wondered how he was even conceived in the first place, how a goddess even fell in love with whoever his father was. He thought of his grandfather, too. The complicated realities overwhelmed him and he sighed again, allowing the full breath to escape this time.

He looked at Kilderan, whose pale blue eyes focused on the wall in front of them, glancing around at the ship's paneling as if it were something more interesting than a mere black surface.

It was only a little while longer before Ganymede came into view, a marble of whites, grays, and tans.

"Let's hope the city has what we need," Aome said, spurring the ship onward.

Rynn glanced at Kilderan and then stood, approaching the cockpit and standing amongst Aome and Yojackson as the window was overwhelmed by the pale sea of the orange, cloud-filled atmosphere.

• • •

Without Yojackson in control of the *Aristarchus*, the landing on Ganymede proceeded unhindered by shaking or thudding or cursing. Although he himself had never flown a ship before, Rynn believed Aome had so far done exceptionally well at navigating the large cargo ship.

He turned to the pilot's seat. "Where did you learn to fly so well?"

Aome eyed him briefly, and then, cocking her head, said, "Lots of experience, I suppose. Out of all the priestesses on Arsteine, I'm certain I made the most journeys that required me to travel by ship rather than speeder."

To Rynn, a celestial priestess was the closest link he had to the goddesses, and he unknowingly felt as if Aome could provide him with information about them. "What did you do at the temple?"

It was a moment before she answered. "There are a lot of people living in Thruhairth's slums. The head priestess, in Arsteine's case Velle Deka, always sends groups of priests and priestesses to help them. But besides that we mostly study the seven empresses and their time among mortals and cling to the hope that one day they will return to their rightful kingdom."

"There aren't many people that actually believe that," Kilderan commented. "There aren't many people who place any trust in our first rulers at all anymore."

Aome shook her head. "It is unfortunate. But at least some of us are doing something to honor their memory." She looked at Rynn. "Saving the forbidden son is the highest honor I could have ever hoped for. The blood of the galaxy's mothers runs through your veins. The blood of the stars. It is incredible that I have had this opportunity." She smiled at Rynn.

Before that declaration, it had not occurred to Rynn how momentous it was for Aome to not only be escorting a son of a celestial goddess across the galaxy but also aiding in his ultimate salvation. It made him feel simultaneously highly significant and increasingly fragile.

The forbidden son. The title unsettled him. It almost sounded like an insult. *What am I, really? Who were my parents, really?* He doubted anyone in the entire galaxy could answer those questions.

"All right!" Yojackson's loud voice crudely shook him from his musings. "How certain are you that Ganymede will have what we need? This could all be a huge waste of time. I know Kip agrees with you, but how are we even going to get ahold of this thing now that we're down there?"

"We will," Aome promised.

"Very reassuring," Yojackson muttered as he opened the ship's ramp and the foursome stepped outside.

It was nearing sunset, and the orange light from the sinking suns shone onto all of their faces. Rynn squinted and Kilderan's hand shot up to block the sunbeams. The glaring light that caught on the ship's metal exterior lessened once they were further from the *Aristarchus*, and Rynn examined the area.

They stood in a mass of golden sand dunes that stretched all the way to the distant horizon and then beyond, an endless expanse. The sky was a pristine, cloudless firmament above them, pulled taut across the heavens. The only sound was the smooth shifting of disturbed sand. The absolute serenity, but mostly the infinitely certain feeling that at that point in time Rynn and his companions were the only living things in the universe made it difficult to believe that not too far away there was a thriving, loud, lively city.

Aome began to move through the sand, which was growing paler and more gray and less golden with the setting suns, saying, "The city is close. It's getting late; we need to hurry."

Night chased them across the dunes, bringing along its smoky purple and blue robes. Rynn gazed up at the arriving stars and the dusky slivers of moons. A breeze ruffled his hair and caused little whirlwinds of sand to be born from the ground. He ran a hand through his hair and glanced back at Kilderan, whose footsteps were nearly unheard in the sea of sand. There was a glow reflecting in his eyes, like that of firelight.

Rynn turned to see the small city before them, where dozens of lanterns had been lit to keep the incoming darkness at bay. A slightly hunched-over man lit them, leaving each golden sphere to mark his route.

Dim shadows moved about in the gloom, entering doors on either side of the street. One or two speeders slowly meandered amongst the pedestrians. The people in the city were of a varied medley of races; the majority contained individuals with scales and horns.

Kilderan's lips parted as he absently scanned the city. "We're going to draw attention. Which is the last thing we need."

"Don't worry," Aome said. "We'll have a place to rest for the night. This city isn't far from the celestial temple of Cinpheron. I am a fellow priestess, so they will welcome us and provide food."

Unlike Port Illuvar, where they brushed shoulders with every visitor, the people of Ganymede's major city Yzhan avoided Rynn, Kilderan, Yojackson, and Aome, some of them even casting almost offended gazes in the travelers' direction. The breeze that had been loitering in the gaps in the dunes seemed to have followed them, and sent a chill across Rynn's skin. He looked over at Yojackson, whose brow was creased, and Aome, who seemed strangely placid in this unfamiliar place, and finally at Kilderan, who walked as if someone was pursuing him. *Because they are.* Rynn tugged at his tunic's sleeves, wishing for a thicker garment or even a robe.

The lanterns flickered lazily, casting a queer yellowish tint onto a group of tall, slender, hooded figures with faces that seemed like they were carved from white stone and who looked to be more like people of the wood rather than a desert planet.

The city seemed increasingly random and out of place, a random collection of various sandstone buildings scattered in the largest gap between the brown dunes, and every passing of the night wind brought more and more coarse sand, as if in protest of the intrusion on the planet's innate solitude.

IX

They had walked for some time, almost going around the city rather than through it, and further into another set of dunes before Aome finally announced that the temple of Cinpheron was near.

Rynn stifled a yawn.

"There it is," Kilderan muttered to him, pointing to the salient building that had no cover whatsoever in the openness of the desert.

Sand had found its way into Rynn's boots, for every time they scaled a dune the sand at its peak would cascade down the surface and into his shoes. He frowned. Glancing to where Kilderan indicated, he saw the cloister was visible ahead.

Rynn gazed up at the marvelous tower, the true temple, which was protected by a collection of smaller white domes that guarded a gargling fountain and the small square surrounding it that was flanked by sandstone sculptures and dead vegetable garden beds. There were more elaborate lanterns lighting up the vicinity, and Rynn caught sight of a few priestesses in white raiment who moved tranquilly about the grounds.

A priestess who looked about Aome's age with honey-colored hair approached them, and the group bowed. "May I help you? Ordinary citizens are not allowed in Empress Cinpheron's temple except on full moon nights."

Aome displayed the string of beads that evidently she carried everywhere and the young priestess' face lit up with recognition and suddenly amiability. "You are a priestess?" She asked, looking over the entire group.

"Yes. I serve Kazari's temple on Arsteine."

"Of course. Why have you come here?"

Aome hesitated, glancing first at Rynn and then at Kilderan, who listed his head. "I am part of an escort to deliver this boy to… to Melerak. We stopped here to refuel and I knew that my fellow celestial priestesses would provide food and lodging."

The girl nodded and gestured for them to follow her into the temple.

Aome stepped in front of Yojackson and Kilderan, further than she already was, and entered the temple.

Intricate carvings and solemn portraits adorned the walls, and tasseled rugs served the same purpose for the floor. A few odd statues and vases of lilies decorated the main room.

The blonde priestess caught a blue-skinned girl by the arm. "Escort these four to their accommodations." She turned to Aome. "We'll deliver food to your room."

Aome nodded. "Thank you."

•••

Rynn bit into one of the large, steaming rolls that the priestesses had brought from the temple's kitchen. His fingers became covered in the bun's glaze.

The room where they had been led to was small with a sand-strewn floor. It had only a bed and a table with two chairs, which were occupied by Rynn and Aome. Leaning against the bedpost was Yojackson, who was picking clean a leg of meat with a gnarled, clawed foot on the end.

"I asked one of the priestesses where their ship maintenance shop is, and it's not far from here," Kilderan was saying, "We can probably walk there in the morning." He moved to the window, where a shaft of moonlight turned his dark tunic silver.

Rynn watched as a ship materialized in the atmosphere, a dark shape amongst the dim stars. He reached for the dish of the odd animal's roasted carcass just as Yojackson did.

"We still don't have any money, though," the criminal reminded him. Turning to Aome, he said, "We're lucky you're a priestess. This food is the best I've had in a while."

"Well, for you this is where the benefits run out," she retorted. "But you are right. I don't know how we'll afford the new jump drive, especially when it's so much of an upgrade from the one the *Aristarchus* has now."

"Well," Yojackson began, "I noticed a couple of *pretty* loaded purses on our way through the city. We could try—"

"We aren't stealing anything," Kilderan interrupted. "We were already being gawked at on our way here, and the last thing we need is to draw more attention to ourselves."

Rynn studied the nicks and gouges in the wooden floor. His head snapped up. "What if we trade the mechanic the drive we've got now in exchange for the new one?"

"That would probably work," Aome said. "The current drive is in good condition."

Rynn mindlessly reached for the plate of glazed rolls, his hand finding only crumbs. He glanced around, wondering if anyone besides himself had actually gotten any.

There was a short silence before Yojackson asked, "Who gets the bed?"

"Rynn." Kilderan replied, gesturing for Rynn to come.

"I figured." The man slumped into the empty chair left by Rynn as the boy made his way to the small, hastily made bed.

Aome joined Kilderan at the window and they both watched as Rynn gingerly settled into the bed under its soft blue quilt. "He is the son of a goddess," Aome muttered. "Technically, he is a prince."

"Thank you for not divulging who we really are," Kilderan said. "I know they are priestesses and therefore the most loyal to the celestial goddesses, but I have never trusted anyone."

Aome dipped her head before cocking it at him. "Where do you come from, anyway? Who are you really? Who is Rynn?"

"I used to live in Thruhairth, but I was staying in the nearest town to Rynn's cottage in the woods when I found him being chased. They were assassins, and they killed his grandfather. Rynn was completely alone in the cottage's closet, and he was injured. That's how I found out he was the son of one of the celestial goddesses. And with all the people, especially on Arsteine, so openly opposed to anything regarding the old empresses' return or their heir, I felt I should protect him."

Aome nodded. "He is very special. And in a lot of danger if in the wrong hands. You did good to rescue him, a complete stranger."

"What else could I have done? A child…A unique child." Kilderan's words ebbed out of Rynn's consciousness as he faded into sleep, wondering the same as Aome and feeling remarkably fortunate to have Kilderan as his companion.

∙ ∙ ∙

"Rynn…wait…no…Dusek… The emperor…why is he…Agh!"

Rynn's eyes fluttered open, the light blushing beams of sunlight hurting them. He squinted. As he absently clutched the pillow beneath his head, he heard groaning.

"The emperor…Blood…I—"

Rynn abruptly sat up, glancing around the room and finding Kilderan amongst an ocean of wadded up sheets on the floor, yet another improvised bed. His hair was a dark mass around his head, a slightly wavy halo lit up by the suns. On his face was a strained expression.

Rynn leaned on one elbow and rubbed his eyes with his other arm, frowning. Kilderan continued to mutter things, but they grew unintelligible. "…Kilderan?"

Yojackson and Aome began to stir and Rynn was about to stand when Kilderan's eyelids reluctantly opened, eerily pale in the cold morning light, and stared drowsily at Rynn. His lips parted.

"Are you all right?" Rynn asked him slowly.

Kilderan craned his neck and scanned Rynn. The suns turned the small scars on his face a pearly hue. But then his eyebrows lowered and he whispered, "What?"

Rynn shoved the blanket off of his legs and slid out of the bed as Kilderan did the same. "You—you were saying things. About me. And the blood."

Kilderan's eyes widened. "What did I say?"

Rynn blinked rapidly a few times. "My name, and the emperor…I don't know."

His shoulders stiffened and he balled up the bedding. He appeared paranoid.

"Is there something you aren't telling me?" Rynn smoothed his hair.

Kilderan shook his head, running a hand over the stubble on his jaw. "It's nothing. Don't worry about it."

∙ ∙ ∙

The suns were still rising when they found the city's ship maintenance station. The building was smaller than Rynn expected. On one side it was flanked by several other storefronts and on the other side a group of large fog harvesting screens that were laden with morning dew. There were two speeders and a rusty, dilapidated fighter ship in front of the garage.

"Don't you think it's a little early in the day for this?" Aome asked as they entered.

"Nope," Yojackson said with his hands on his hips, for inside were multiple patrons lingering near sparsely stocked shelves and talking in a subdued tone.

Aome frowned. "I wasn't asking you."

No one inside the garage wore clothing that could have even remotely marked him as a mechanic, and the four outsiders began to examine the area, confused, as they moved past the entrance.

Soon they encountered a grimy desk, with a turned back behind it.

"No, I don't have the parts you—Well, I *have* them, but there ain't no way I'm deliverin' a couple pieces o' junk to you when you're so far outside o' the city, 'specially with all those pirates and bounty hunters runnin' around lately. Oh, of course, threaten to withhold the payment! I'll withhold the parts, and your fancy little cycle won't be goin' to no races!"

"Are you the mechanic around here?" Yojackson asked, leaning on the counter.

"Eh?" The stranger turned around, revealing himself to be a tall, muscular, blue-skinned man with tangled hair and a greasy tunic. "I am the mechanic around here. What do you want?"

Kilderan stepped forward after exchanging doubtful glances with Aome. "We need a jump drive, far faster than the one we have now, a two hundred MLS."

The man scratched his head. "How much faster?"

"We plan on upgrading to a five hundred MLS."

The mechanic's brows shot up and he began to shake his head, but then stopped. "Well, I was about to say I couldn't help you, but I'm pretty sure I've got a four hundred MLS, if you'll take that one."

Kilderan looked at Aome, who nodded.

"Well, then, how much have you got? Such an increase in jump speed won't be cheap."

"We don't have any money," Kilderan explained.

"But," Yojackson interrupted, stepping forward and causing his earrings to clink together noisily, "We can bargain."

The man frowned.

"Would you be willing to accept our current jump drive? It's in perfect condition," the criminal continued.

"I get a lot o' customers comin' in here needin' stuff like that, so I'd be obliged, but it still won't cut it." He squinted. "So unless you've got something else…" He reached for a thin metal box, which he handed off to a customer who dropped credits onto the counter.

"What about those parts you need delivered?" Kilderan piped up. "We could make that run for you."

"So you're an eavesdroppin' lot, eh?"

"We didn't mean to pry," Aome protested.

"Ah, never mind." He leaned closer to Kilderan. "Are you sure you'd be able to do that? This pain in the neck lives way out in the middle o' nowhere, an' a lot o' bandits have been ambushing the roads lately."

"You would give us the drive?"

He nodded.

"Then we'll do it."

"Wait, Kilderan…Are you sure?" Aome caught him by the arm.

"There isn't any other way to get that jump drive without wasting more time than we can afford. We have to."

• • •

The wind whipped at Rynn's hair and he squinted against the bright daylight coming from the suns that were now directly overhead. He gripped the edge of the bouncing speeder lent to them by the mechanic, his eyes scanning the horizon for anything besides the monotonous scenery of sand and the disappearing city behind them. He tugged at the hood of his brown robe, a garment given to all of them by the priestesses to offer them some protection from the relentless suns. It was a little large for his head, and often fell into his face and obscured his vision. The sleeves, too, coupled with the length of his tunic sleeves, made for an altogether awkward and bulky garb. The suns glinted on the speeder and Rynn squeezed his eyes shut.

"Where is this place, anyway?" he shouted over the rumbling vehicle.

Yojackson, who was driving, glanced back at him and the hovering speeder swerved. "What?"

The wind threatening to throw Rynn's hood back from his head and he put one hand on it to keep it in place. "I said, how far are we?"

"Oh! Not too far, according to these coordinates the ship mechanic gave us!"

Rynn, still squinting, glanced around at the rusty speeder bed and at Kilderan and Aome, who were gripping the sides of the speeder like Rynn to steady the jarring ride.

Rynn pulled at his boots and his face wrinkled up at the sand scratched his skin.

"Up ahead!" Yojackson called as the speeder leapt in the air over a pothole in the already crudely built, if not nearly nonexistent, road.

Rynn looked up and saw a shape almost materialize on the horizon, a deep brown smudge that wavered in his vision due to the heat.

"It won't be too far, now," Kilderan said, his voice raised.

There was suddenly a loud explosion and the speeder lurched forward, throwing the three passengers out of their positions. They all looked back to see a mass of smoke curling into the air. Rynn's head snapped up and he saw three larger speeders pursuing their own. Multiple men in shabby clothing and dirty leather jackets and large goggles stood on each one, waving swords and guns in the air. He noticed one with a large rifle who was likely the reason for their speeder's smoke.

"The bandits!" Kilderan called, gripping Yojackson's seat. "Go faster, Jack!"

The bandits aimed at their speeder again and a few bullets plinked against the metal. The speeder veered to one side.

The bandits' speeders accelerated and a few brave pirates leapt from their large vehicles onto the one lent to Rynn and his companions.

"Blast it!" Yojackson released his control over the speeder and turned around with a pistol in one hand. He fired, and one of the bandits cried out before falling off of the rickety speeder into the sand.

Kilderan, too, had brandished his weapon, though he had yet to use it, and was shoving a bandit off of the speeder. Another round of shots resounded throughout the dunes and Yojackson did the same as him.

Rynn turned to the horizon. There was a small sand-colored dome rapidly approaching. He turned back to the raiders, frowning when he saw that their speeders were slowing and turning to retreat. He glanced at Yojackson, who was back at the helm of the speeder, and then at Aome and Kilderan, who were as concerned as he was.

A small, blue fighter craft was hovering near their speeder, its guns whirring.

"What's going on?" Rynn yelled.

They had reached their destination and Yojackson halted the speeder a little way away from the pod house.

The fighter ship gingerly flew away and landed even more carefully next to the house.

Yojackson slid out of the speeder and helped Rynn to dismount it. The four then approached the blue ship.

A man with a row of small, yellowed horns wearing a strange set of sand-covered armor emerged from its cockpit. He held an arm up.

"Who are you?" Kilderan asked as the man neared them.

He gazed past them at the speeder, which was still discharging exhaust. "I could've helped you a lot sooner if I had the ship fixed." He glared at Kilderan rather harshly. "Who are *you*?"

"Actually, we are the ones sent to deliver those ship parts," Kilderan said, glancing at Yojackson, who trotted over to the speeder and removed a net filled with odd ship components that jangled as he returned and handed it to the man. "So, if you'll hand over the payment, we'll be leaving."

The man glanced around again, growing distant, thinking. Rynn peered at him and he frowned back. "I don't think so, son." He produced a small metal orb from the folds of his armor and turned it on. A hologram flickered to life.

Kilderan's eyes widened, along with every one of his companions'. The hologram depicted Kilderan's own face, features placid and eyes cold, beneath lines of text labeling him as highly wanted, alive, for a large payment. "How…" He began.

The man raised his eyebrows as he pressed the projector's button again, and Kilderan's picture disappeared to reveal Yojackson's slightly smirking face with the same instructions.

"Well, blast it," Yojackson muttered.

"I'm about to get a lot of rounds of drinks, and a new set of armor." The man pulled out a gun that appeared to be charred and chipped at. "Especially when the bounties have been issued by Emperor Dusek himself."

Rynn's lips parted and he began to back away. He looked over at Kilderan, who seemed to have completely frozen and melted away, simultaneously.

"Emperor Dusek…" Yojackson began, "I've never had the honor, unless you count a brief run-in when I was attempting theft of some palace riches, but I hear he's quite a pain in the back for people like me. I—"

The man fired his weapon into the air. "Drop your guns."

Yojackson held up his hands in submission and reached for his pistol. He pulled it from its holster and fired at the bounty hunter. The man fell to the ground with a thud. Yojackson stooped down to the body and tore the purse off of the man's waist with a scoff.

Rynn watched as Kilderan swallowed hard and panted lightly, touching a hand briefly to his neck. He turned to Rynn. "They know where we are. They know where you are. They—"

"Hold it right there!" someone called as a group of men dressed in the same manner as the bounty hunter rushed out of the domed house.

"Get to the speeder!" Kilderan yelled before mumbling, "Blast it."

They obeyed and rushed towards the broken vehicle. Rynn heard Kilderan cry out and stumble, clutching his leg. "Kilderan!"

He lifted himself off of the ground and limped past Rynn. "Go! Get to the speeder!"

"What's going on?"

Rynn heard the bounty hunters shouting. "Don't kill 'im, blast it!"

"One shot to the leg ain't gonna kill 'im, you imbecile! After them! This'll be the largest bounty in my entire life!"

Aome rushed over to Rynn and they assisted Kilderan in clambering into the speeder, Kilderan's fist painfully clutching Rynn's shoulder.

Yojackson was already waiting in the driver's seat, aiming his pistol at the hunters. "I've got one of them, now hurry before we have to deal with more!"

Kilderan grunted as he landed in the speeder and Aome and Rynn barely steadied themselves before the speeder lurched and raced away at its highest speed.

"You all right, Kip?" Yojackson yelled.

Kilderan gripped his thigh. "Just get us back to the city."

"We need to tear open the leg of your trousers and look at the wound," Aome said.

"No!" Kilderan said, stifling a groan. "I can deal with it once we get back to the temple."

"We need to see how bad the wound is *now*," Aome insisted.

Kilderan stared at Rynn, his eyes darting around the boy's distressed face.

"Come on, Kilderan," Rynn said. "Why can't we look at it?"

Kilderan leaned against the wall of the speeder, grimacing.

"The bullet must've really lodged itself in there," Aome said, reaching for Kilderan's leg.

He tried to shake his head, but instead his jaw and the tendons in his neck tightened. "There's something—"

Aome pulled an exceptionally small knife out of her jacket and tore Kilderan's black trousers. She hissed. "It almost went all the way through your leg. How—" Her jaw fell.

Rynn's eyes widened as he looked upon the bullet injury. A strange current ran through him. He glanced up into Kilderan's icy eyes and blinked back his distress.

The blood flooding his thigh gleamed with an ethereal sheen.

X

By the time their speeder had hurriedly made its way back through the city and to the temple the three suns were setting and night had returned for another pursuit. Rynn focused on keeping his eyes locked on the heavens and the glorious yellow sky that was evanescent, dwindling like everything else had ever since the day of Asold's death. His thoughts were an incomprehensible tangle and Kilderan's rapid breathing so close to him sent a sting into his chest.

I am not the only forbidden son. The image of Kilderan's blood, scarlet and glistening, overtook Rynn's mind and he blinked slowly, the sky blurring in his eyelashes. He looked down at his feet and at the tip of Kilderan's boot out of the corner of his eye. *Forbidden sons of goddesses and mortals.*

He shifted, uncomfortable, and turned back to the sky, strangely clear and illuminated though dusk was rapidly approaching.

"How is he?" Yojackson asked, turning around in the driver's seat.

"We're hanging in here." Aome tossed her loosely braided blush-colored hair over her shoulder. "Can't you make this piece of junk go any faster?"

"This is as fast as she gets, sister. Unfortunately she isn't exactly the latest model."

Rynn released an anxious breath and turned from the firmament to his companions. "Hurry, Yojackson!"

"It's fine, I'm fine," Kilderan said.

"There's a bullet in your leg and you're bleeding out," Aome deadpanned. "You're not fine."

Yojackson turned the speeder as they came to the temple and Rynn was certain it was going to overturn and they were all going to fall into the sand.

"Go faster but don't get us killed!" Aome exclaimed.

Rynn heard an irritated sigh come from Yojackson as he inched closer to Kilderan.

Yojackson parked the speeder and practically jumped out of it. "We need to get him inside. Someone's going to have to remove that bullet."

Aome and Rynn turned and stared at him in unison.

The criminal spread his palms and raised his eyebrows. "Okay then."

All three of them aided in carrying Kilderan through the temple, encountering almost no priestesses except for those who had not retired for the evening who looked on in curiosity and offered declined help.

Yojackson plowed into the door to the room they were staying in and he and Aome laid Kilderan on the bed.

"I'm fine," he said again.

"Not for much longer," Yojackson warned. "The adrenaline is gonna leave you any minute now. Help him roll onto his stomach, priestess."

"Do you have pliers?" she asked.

He fished into one of the sheaths on his belt. "Grabbed them from the speeder," he said, holding it up so that it glinted in the light coming through the window.

Aome bit her lip.

He moved towards Kilderan and tore open the leg of his pants. He bent so that he was almost eye level with his friend. "This is going to hurt, Kip."

Rynn glimpsed his flesh, reddened and covered in shimmering scarlet blood. He watched as Yojackson carefully moved the pair of pliers towards Kilderan's leg.

"Careful!" Aome warned.

As soon as the tool touched Kilderan's wound, just barely brushing against the deep injury, an agonizing scream tore from his lips.

Rynn winced.

Yojackson wet his lips and then squinted, the pliers slowly disappearing into the bullet wound.

Kilderan groaned and screamed again.

Rynn felt odd gaping at the deep, bloodied cavity and Yojackson's rough hands holding onto the grimy plier handles protruding from the injury in Kilderan's bruised thigh. His body seized up and he turned away, brushing his damp hair off of his forehead.

"The longer the bullet is in there, the worse he will be," Aome said.

"I know that. But I can't just dig in there." Yojackson exhaled and wriggled the pliers deeper into the skin, eliciting another shriek from Kilderan.

Rynn seated himself at the table and watched Kilderan's fist clenching the sheets.

"I think I found the bullet," Yojackson announced.

Rynn stared down at his hands and tapped his fingers against themselves. His spine tingled and he felt very unusual. He dared to glance back at the bed where Yojackson's amateur operation was taking place. Kilderan's jaw was clenched. Aome had given him a rag to bite into.

"I've got it," the criminal muttered. He gingerly pulled the pliers from Kilderan's leg, and to Rynn it seemed an eternity before the head of the pliers was visible.

The pliers slipped. "Blast it."

A muffled scream.

Yojackson examined the pliers. The bullet was minuscule and colored a sparkling crimson shade. "Let's bandage him up."

•••

"Rest here for a while," Aome said as she helped Kilderan onto his back. She whipped her head around to face Yojackson, craning her neck, for she only stood as tall as the tip of his nose. "Are you sure you did that correctly?"

"The bullet's out, isn't it?"

"You know what I mean. What if he limps for the rest of his life?"

"At least he's alive. You're fortunate that I actually had the backbone to remove the blasted thing."

"We are a peaceful priestess and a child. What do you expect, pirate?"

Yojackson smirked.

Aome turned away from him.

Yojackson sauntered over to Rynn. "If I didn't know any better, I'd say I'm beginning to grow on her."

Without turning, Aome retorted, "You *don't* know any better."

∙∙∙

The night passed without any more events, and by the time Rynn awoke in the morning, Aome and Yojackson were already roused and studying the sleeping Kilderan.

Rynn rolled up his bedding and sat at the table.

Kilderan shifted in the bed, blinking his eyes open and silently listening to Aome.

"The other priestesses want to know what's going on, but I won't let them see you. Not too closely, anyway." Aome glanced at Yojackson, who rested his thumbs in the loops of his belt, but she avoided Rynn's gaze.

This is why he knows so much about the celestial blood. This is why he is so desperate to protect me. This is why… He dropped his gaze to the floor and set to removing his boots, wincing and fighting back a hiss as he looked upon all of the reddened blisters covering his feet.

"What about the jump drive?" Yojackson asked Aome.

She pressed her lips together. "You still have that purse?"

He nodded.

"Then we'll pay for it out of that." She turned back to Kilderan. "We'll install the jump drive into the ship, so we can leave once you've recovered a little."

He said nothing, and Aome and Yojackson deserted the room.

Rynn kept his eyes lowered, but he could hear the bed creak as Kilderan shifted and the sound of the young man's toes tapping idly against the end of the bed.

"Rynn." His voice was low and raspy.

A chill ran through Rynn's body. He looked at Kilderan, who was leaning his head against the mountain of pillows Aome had provided him. Rynn stood.

"You...You have the celestial blood." Rynn swallowed, nearing Kilderan. He furrowed his brow when he noticed Kilderan's eyes were glistening. There was a bright, saturated, golden glow from the rising suns filling the room, making the sparkling blood on Kilderan's newly bandaged thigh even more obvious.

"How does the blood make you feel, Rynn?"

Rynn frowned, trying to shift his attention to a scar on Kilderan's cheek rather than his overwhelming blue eyes. Eventually he answered, "...Heavy. Foreign, almost, I suppose. And scared. I'm so scared, Kilderan. Ever since the day my grandfather died..." His voice hiccuped.

"I understand." He lowered his gaze to his thigh. He patted the spot beside where he sat. Rynn joined him with a clenched stomach.

Rynn stared at Kilderan's wounded thigh and the rapidly staining bandage. He looked at Kilderan.

"Our veins are more abundant than any mortal's and bleed so much more freely. That's why—" He paused and stared out the window.

Rynn sighed.

Neither of them said a word, and it seemed they barely even breathed, for what seemed like an eon. The sunbeams bounced around the room. Rynn's veins droned.

Finally, Rynn felt he had to break the silence. "Then you are one of the celestial goddesses' son, too. Whoever our mothers were..."

Kilderan suddenly sat up, his injured leg a useless, dead weight. He clasped Rynn's hand. "Not mothers, Rynn. *Mother.* Zelia was your mother, as well as mine. We are brothers, Rynn." His eyes were tearful.

Rynn's lungs exhaled the pent-up breath for him and his shoulders slumped. "You're my brother...?"

"That is the real reason I came for you. That's why I want to keep you safe." To himself he muttered, "I want to keep you safe so badly."

Rynn's eyes filled with tears that he did not try to blink away. "You're my brother. I have a brother. Kilderan—"

Kilderan released Rynn's hand to cup his face. He leaned forward and then bent, placing a chaste kiss against the boy's forehead. When he stared into Rynn's large brown eyes again there was a sort of tranquility about his features.

Rynn felt more tears roll in rivulets down his flushed cheeks and abruptly embraced Kilderan, his arms tight around the young man's waist. He buried his face in the black tunic, Kilderan returning the gesture.

But then Rynn released him. Rynn sat back and looked up into Kilderan's eyes. "Who is our father?" he asked.

"We…" Kilderan glanced away for a half second. "We do not share a father."

"Who is *my* father?"

"I—I don't know."

Rynn frowned and clenched his jaw. "Who—Who is *your* father, Kilderan?" He was growing very confused.

"I don't know," Kilderan said, almost a whisper.

Rynn's voice adopted the same tone. "Why didn't you tell me?"

"I tried to, I did. Multiple times. I just…It was never the right time, I…" He winced, though not from the pain of his wound. "I am afraid, Rynn. Possibly more than you are. Yes, more. I have always been afraid. And until we make it to the spring where flesh and blood become light and fire, I will be afraid every moment. I really wanted to tell you, from the first day I saw you. It was only that—"

"It doesn't matter," Rynn lied. He forced a half-smile.

Kilderan lowered his head and then looked at Rynn through the veil of dark brown hair that fell into his face. He leaned forward again and wrapped his arms around Rynn. His lips brushed against Rynn's ear as he said, "I'm sorry, Rynn. I'm sorry I'm afraid. I'm sorry you're afraid. I…" His voice was choked.

Rynn sniffed and embraced him. "It's ok, Kilderan." He paused before adding, "It's ok, brother."

Rynn sniffed again and Kilderan exhaled, echoing in a breathy voice, "Brother. My brother."

...

Kilderan's blue eyes kept darting to the view the window provided: the racing clouds and the unusually frequent arrival of fighter ships and the infrequent—as was expected—sight of leaving ships. He soundlessly took occasional sips from the bowl of broth Aome and Yojackson had returned with.

"This has set us back a few days," Yojackson pointed out, holding a bowl of broth like Kilderan's, though any drink he took was a noisy slurp. He swiveled his head to look at Aome. "So much for saving time."

She furrowed her brow. "None of us knew that this was going to happen."

Rynn did not say the words that sprang into his mind. *Yeah. None of us had any idea.* He was not angry with Kilderan, but the surprise and mystification that now occupied his mind served to make him, in a way, bashful and uncertain towards Kilderan, as if the reserved, apprehensive young man's thoughts did not already elude Rynn.

But holding his words back did not prevent Aome from stepping forward. "Now that you've started to heal, Kilderan, answer me this: When did you plan on telling us that you, too, are a son of another celestial goddess? How is that even possible? I was told there was only one forbidden son that disappeared ages ago." She glanced at Rynn.

Kilderan lowered his dish. "Not *another* celestial goddess."

Aome lowered her angled pink brows even further. Her confused expression passed between Kilderan and Rynn, and then to Kilderan again, and once more to Rynn. "You two are *related*?"

Rynn nodded timidly.

Kilderan returned to the tureen in his hands.

Yojackson set his bowl on the table and leaned against the wall. He sighed loudly and in a nonchalant voice he said, "About time, Kip."

Aome's braid whipped around furiously as she spun towards Yojackson. "You *knew*? Why *you* of all people?"

Yojackson smirked, winked, but did not answer her.

She turned to Kilderan and Rynn, her face bewildered and seeking an explanation.

"Jack knew me when I was very young. I—"

"Aome," Rynn interrupted, "I didn't know. He only told me a few days ago." He glanced, worried, at Kilderan, who averted the gaze Rynn could feel resting on his neck.

Aome sighed. *"Two* sons?" She clasped a hand to her chin in thought as she slowly seated herself at the table. "I am in the presence of two celestial children."

"I take it this is a pretty high honor for you, priestess. You see—"

"Jack." Kilderan's stare bore into Yojackson's questioning face. The same look they had shared while being held hostage by the pirates at the abandoned spaceport was exchanged between them.

Rynn frowned.

Yojackson ducked his head.

Kilderan drew everyone's attention as he shifted in the bed with a groan. He gaped back at them for a moment before saying, "We should leave. We should get to the ship and get off of this planet."

"What about your leg?" Aome asked.

He shook his head. "We've wasted enough time already. And word is bound to spread of what happened during that ship parts delivery."

"Are you sure?"

Yojackson shoved himself off of the wall and came to stand beside Aome. "He's right. Whatever we decide to do next, we should at least be drifting through space while we make the decision, not in the largest, most prominent building in the entire city."

"Help me stand," Kilderan muttered.

Yojackson grabbed Kilderan's black coat from the end of the bed and then approached the side of the bed and stooped, wrapping an arm around Kilderan's back.

"What if someone sees us leaving?" Rynn questioned.

"Just ignore them. It's none of their business what we do," Yojackson replied, garnering a frown from Aome, who joined him in helping Kilderan limp out of the room.

Rynn followed closely behind, wincing every time Kilderan whimpered and assured them he was fine. His fingertips and tongue stung as if he had just consumed the celestial blood, and amidst his absent thought he bit into the side of his cheek and stifled a cry.

The hallway was better lit by the sunlight streaming in through the windows than it was by the wavering candles inside the lanterns hanging at intervals on the walls. No priestesses stopped them on their way out of the temple, and soon they felt the suns burning into their backs.

Rynn wrinkled his nose and squinted his eyes, the sand dunes blindingly white in the daylight.

"Blast it," Yojackson said under his breath. "The ship is all the way through the city. We can't have you walk that entire way—" Suddenly, a chuckle escaped him. "We won't need to."

Rynn and Aome turned to where he looked, his eyes twinkling. A small speeder, even smaller than the one loaned to them for the delivery, sat before the temple's entrance. It was filled with crates whose contents were only shadows against the crates' walls.

"I will *not* steal a speeder from a *celestial temple*." Aome released her hold on Kilderan and stepped away from him and Yojackson.

"Ah, it's not *so* illegal," Yojackson assured her, "And speaking of sort-of-illegal things, I don't know much about the creed of the celestial followers, but I'd like to know why *you* were in a tavern instead of a temple, priestess. And besides, the celestial children are in on it, so lighten up."

Aome glared at him, but her chagrin was ignored as the criminal helped Kilderan into the speeder and seated himself in the driver's seat. Rynn skirted Aome and situated himself next to Kilderan, who seemed tired but hopeful.

Yojackson cackled and the speeder suddenly lurched forward, throwing them out of their seats. The dunes became a blurred smear of gold along either side of Rynn's vision, and with every mound they crested the speeder threatened to fly into the air, only to come crashing down onto the land again.

"You couldn't have done this when it was an emergency?" Aome shouted, gripping the speeder's wall.

"I had to be careful then. But this one's stolen."

The city stood before them and continued to grow closer as the rumble of the engine filled Rynn's ears. Aome shouted something to Yojackson, but it was incoherent and all Rynn could hear was more cackling from the criminal at the helm.

A cloud of dust and sand burst from the ground as the speeder barely dodged the bank of a dune. A few armored citizens jumped out of the way as the speeder turned a corner.

"Hey!" one of them yelled. "Isn't that one of our bounties?"

"Yojackson Owens!" called the other.

Yojackson turned and saluted the two men but swore as a hooded woman pulled a rifle from its holster. Rynn was quickly reminded of their chase with the bandits as the bullets sped into the sand behind them.

Yojackson evaded a few more buildings before racing out of the city altogether and into the barren desert beyond.

They reached the sunbeam-tipped crowns of a few more dunes when finally the *Aristarchus* came into view amongst a ring of hills. Yojackson turned almost completely around in his seat to be certain their pursuers had given up and the speeder collided with a decently sized dune. They were all thrown from the vehicle and Rynn, Aome, and Kilderan cried out.

It was a few heartbeats before they recovered and Yojackson helped Kilderan to stand and Aome came to Rynn's aid. Gazing upon the smoking speeder, the criminal scratched his shaved head and then shrugged, making his way over to the ship.

"Everyone inside," Yojackson ordered, dropping the *Aristarchus*' ramp. "Let's get out of this dump."

XI

"I always hated sand," Yojackson grumbled, shaking sand from his long maroon jacket before shoving his arms through its sleeves. "All right," he said loudly, sauntering up to the cockpit and collapsing into the pilot's seat. "Priestess, will you be my copilot?"

"I have a name, you know, pirate," Aome spat. But even as she did, she slowly made her way to the seat next to him.

He raised an eyebrow. "Really?"

Rynn sat next to Kilderan and sighed as a feeling of security came over him, from being back on the ship that had enveloped him in its slightly busted metal walls so many times, shielding him from whatever danger he had just escaped. But the security was replaced with discomfort and anxiety as he realized just how much trouble he and his companions had gotten into ever since Kilderan had spirited him away from the clearing in the forest, the only place he had ever known.

Kilderan. My brother. He's much older than I am...Where was he all those years? Why didn't Grandfather protect him, too? He stole a glance at Kilderan, who was examining his dressed leg with an expression that to Rynn seemed like he was not gazing at the leg at all.

Rynn reluctantly reached for Kilderan's sleeve and tugged at it. The young man's head snapped up and his pupils widened, two unreadable black abysses inside two pale oceans, and altogether melancholy.

"Are you okay?" Rynn asked.

Kilderan nodded stiffly. "Are you?"

"I'm scared," Rynn whispered.

Kilderan cocked his head.

"We're going back to Arsteine, and—"

"Me too," his brother whispered back. "But I will do everything in my power not to let the emperor find you." He hesitated before adding, "Find *us*." He blinked. "I'm not so certain it's even a good idea anymore."

"What?" Aome turned as she released her hold on the copilot's controls.

"Should we even return to Arsteine? You saw how much trouble we got into on Ganymede."

"Yeah, and about those bounties…" Yojackson began.

Kilderan sat forward. "I don't know what to make of those. I have no idea how the emperor even placed a bounty on my head, or knew where we were, or how such a distant, underpopulated planet received the orders so fast. Yojackson I can understand, but—"

Yojackson's mouth fell open and he drew back, feigning offense. But then he resumed his previous position, this time resting his chin on one hand. He thought for a long moment before saying, "A tracking device."

"What?"

"They must be tracking us somehow. How do you think they knew our location so quickly and accurately?" He glanced around at the ship, looking paranoid. "It must be somewhere on the ship."

"How would they implant a tracking device? When have we—" Aome squinted. "Port Illuvar?"

Yojackson started to speak, but was interrupted by Kilderan.

The young man shook his head. "An imperial ship found us right before we decided to go to the spaceport for repairs. But you're right, Aome." He furrowed his brow.

A wave of anxiety came over Rynn. *If we're being tracked, are Kilderan's efforts all for nothing? Why hasn't the emperor come for us already? Maybe…* The thought nearly suffocated him. Inhaling, he opened his mouth to speak, but withdrew. His eyes darted to Kilderan and then away from his brother and he decided to voice his notion. "Maybe the emperor isn't tracking the *ship*. Maybe he's tracking me." He glanced at Kilderan, who scratched at his neck and toyed for a brief instant with the short hair at the nape. "Maybe that's how the assassins found me."

No one spoke, and Rynn guessed it was because he was so likely to be correct.

"Well, there's not much we can do about that, if you're right." Yojackson leaned back into the pilot's seat as they drifted above Ganymede.

"We don't know for sure if we're even being tracked at all," Aome reminded them. "But I think we should keep with our plan to return to Arsteine." In response to the skeptical expressions that suddenly lit up everyone's faces, she said, "I know that basically every scoundrel in the galaxy is looking for us, and that Arsteine could possibly be the worst place to go right now, but if even the remote planets have heard of us, we aren't safe on any of the planets or spaceports anyway."

"She's right. You're right. We can't give up the journey to Velle Deka that easily." Kilderan folded his arms across his chest and glanced around at each one of them through a lock of dark hair that had fallen into his face. "How long does the ship estimate it will take for us to reach Arsteine?"

Aome turned to Yojackson.

He shifted his attention to the controls. "Ah…Here we are." He turned back to Kilderan. "Only a few days. And one stop at a spaceport, maybe. Not like that will be a problem now." He unlatched and dangled the bounty hunter's coin pouch in the air. "That guy was loaded."

"All right," Aome said. "…Setting a course for the capital planet Arsteine. We're going home."

Kilderan seemed to tense up at Aome's words, and he glimpsed Rynn in the corner of his eye as the stars blurred as the familiar jump through space began.

• • •

"Rynn."

Something nudged his shoulder blade.

"Rynn…"

There was a gentle, careful touch on his shoulder.

"Rynn, wake up."

The blackness dispersed as Rynn's eyes fluttered open. There was a pain in his back from lying on the hard bench of the ship. He did not even remember falling asleep.

"Rynn." Kilderan's voice was right next to his ear.

He abruptly sat up, his head swimming. He turned and saw his brother sitting in the same place as he had been before Rynn had fallen asleep. Rynn rubbed his eyes, feeling unusually exhausted.

"We're one jump away," Kilderan said. He inclined his head. "You fell asleep on me."

Rynn blinked and then squinted at him, recoiling slightly. "We're really going back?"

It was a few moments before Kilderan nodded.

"But what about what you told me? The emperor? My blood…" His eyes widened and then he grew somber. "Won't Emperor Dusek want to find you, too? You have the celestial blood, too. Kilderan, what—"

Kilderan quieted him as Rynn felt fear swelling inside of himself. "What did I tell you? The emperor will never find you. That's what I'm here for." He placed a hand on Rynn's shoulder.

Rynn suddenly felt compelled to embrace his brother, and he did. He tried to breathe. "You said the emperor will do terrible things to me if he finds us. I'm scared. I don't want to put any of you in any danger because the emperor is after me."

Kilderan said nothing, and stared down at the tip of his boot. He sighed. "One more jump," he muttered, mostly to himself.

• • •

Arsteine appeared different to Rynn than it had looked the first time he had ever seen it. It seemed almost foreign, a pearl that trapped the swirling clouds beneath its clear atmosphere hanging in the ink-black void and staring down at the cargo ship that it dwarfed.

Yojackson swiveled in his chair. "What's your plan for once we make it down there? None of us are exactly welcome on Arsteine."

Kilderan pressed his lips into a firm line, a small white scar above his mouth pulled taut.

"We head for Kazari's temple. Velle Deka will be there, along with all of my celestial sisters." A small smile came to her lips. "They will be even more welcoming than the priestesses at Cinpheron's temple."

Rynn stared past Aome and Yojackson at Arsteine, thinking of his grandfather and of the emperor he knew he was supposed to fear so much. He was cautious and wary of Emperor Dusek but did not fear him with every fiber of his being, and he figured it was because he really did not understand what Kilderan spoke of. He had no inkling of what Arsteine's ruler was truly like anymore, originally supposing him to be the benevolent leader everyone knew him as. But he trusted Kilderan. "I'm ready to go," he said, smiling.

Aome's own smile widened and Yojackson raised his eyebrows and his lips parted. Kilderan's throat was stiff as he swallowed, and he stared as Rynn had done at the planet in front of them.

"Heading for the city," Yojackson said, turning back to the cockpit window.

"No," Aome said. "They'll be able to see us entering the atmosphere, and if we are being tracked we don't want to go immediately to our destination. Land in the outskirts of Thruhairth."

"You can't head for the city!" Kilderan protested.

"It's the only place where we can legally, safely land. And where they would least expect to see us. Besides, the palace only overlooks the capital city from a distance. Trust us, Kilderan." Aome tugged the band from her pink locks and focused on rearranging the hair.

"It'll be fine, Kip," Yojackson assured him. He stood and stepped towards Kilderan, kneeling to almost be at eye level with the seated man. He dropped his voice into a mutter. "Remember who you're doing this for. If you want to save him, you'll have to take a couple risks and get into a little danger in order to avoid something much, much worse. I myself have had thoughts of how likely I am to be imprisoned again for gallivanting across the galaxy with you three, but you helped me once, Kip, and if I don't help an innocent child stay safe, it kind of makes me look like an ungrateful snake." He clapped a hand onto Kilderan's shoulder and the young man stiffened. "I am a lot of things, but a snake isn't *necessarily* one of them, and though I hate to admit it, there is some sort of distorted moral compass somewhere deep inside of me."

Kilderan laughed quietly and shook his head.

"…and I am very grateful for that day. I mean, the kind of offense I was making spelled a death sentence for sure, knowing how Dusek runs this place."

After a moment of hesitation, Kilderan slowly clutched Yojackson's hand on his shoulder. "Thank you, Jack. I know I'm not exactly a strong person, I've realized that, especially because I have to be strong to protect Rynn. And sometimes I fear I won't be able to do it and he—" He lowered his gaze.

"You're trying. You care what happens to him. Therefore, you are strong enough." Yojackson sighed and stifled a roll of his eyes. "See? I told you I have some kind of compass."

Kilderan looked up at him and smiled again. He clasped Yojackson's hand in his and craned his neck. "Yeah, Aome. Go ahead. Go to Thruhairth."

Yojackson sprang up, dashed past Rynn, and joined her in the cockpit.

•••

Rynn's vision blurred for an instant, so brief that he barely noticed, and he had the sensation that he had just opened his eyes from a long, drowsy sleep. His veins burned, always unsettling him because he was so aware of their existence. There was a peculiar feeling behind his sternum, odd in its familiarity and vagueness both.

He glanced up at Kilderan, who sat stiffer than Rynn himself, tapping his boot against the floor of the *Aristarchus*. "I feel…strange," he said in explanation of the questioning look his brother gave him. He shook his head. "I can't explain it. It's familiar, but totally strange. I—"

"I think I know what you mean."

Rynn furrowed his brow and studied Kilderan's drifting gaze, puzzled.

"I…sense something," Kilderan continued. "How far are we into the atmosphere?"

"Just entered it," Yojackson replied.

Kilderan turned back to Rynn. "I—"

"It's probably nothing," Rynn put in.

"If we both feel it, it's not nothing," Kilderan said. He glanced around, thinking. Soon his head snapped up, though he had completely disregarded the odd perception. "Yojackson, can you try to fly somewhere outside of the usual routes? There are far too many ships way too close to us."

"The legal landing area is just up ahead," Aome told him.

"We're trying to go in undetected, priestess," Yojackson said, leaning his head to one side. "There's nothing legal about any of this."

Rynn looked and saw that Kilderan was correct: the cockpit window that normally displayed a clear swathe of sky was now crowded with a stream of cargo ships and fighters, a torrent that the *Aristarchus* was part of. The assemblage of glinting metal in a variety of colors faded away as the ship veered to the side and deserted it.

Thruhairth was sprawled out below them, and its scenery grew more and more visible as they began to land. There were spiraling buildings and colorful banners and strangely dressed personages and sleek racing cycles and light fighter ships hovering above the streets. Port Illuvar was nothing compared to the capital, Rynn thought, and it amazed him that such a huge, hectic city existed so close to his home in comparison to everywhere he had been that seemed years away in distance now that he was finally on his home planet once again.

The ship made contact with the ground, obscured by other parked vessels but still a ways from the actual landing area.

"Well, we're here," Yojackson announced as Aome left her seat and Rynn stood abruptly, his veins still pulsing.

Kilderan did not stand, and seemed cemented to his seat. His hands were folded, his elbows on his thighs, and one anxious finger curled in and out idly. He swallowed.

"Kilderan?" Rynn stepped away from where the others drew dark hoods over their heads and stood next to Kilderan, their knees almost touching.

Kilderan's tongue wetted his lips.

Rynn looked down at Kilderan, his hair falling into his eyes and obscuring his vision.

The young man slowly lifted his head, his glistening gaze soft and meek, and then his eyes met Rynn's. "Let's go find Velle Deka," he said, the ghost of a smile caressing his face but not reaching his eyes.

They joined Aome and Yojackson in donning black cloaks.

• • •

The suns were glaringly bright as they stepped out of the dark metal shell that was the *Aristarchus*. Rynn's hood greatly reduced his field of vision, but he could feel the others brushing up against him as their wary company trotted through the outskirts of Thruhairth.

The noise of the civilization hammered itself into Rynn's ears, ears that were more accustomed to the silence of the woods. There were a myriad ships overhead, transports beside, and he was certain even the ground rumbled. They continued to move through the city and the outskirts gradually changed to better suit their name, growing slightly more peaceful.

"Um," Yojackson said, "Up ahead."

They looked at his discreet gesture and saw a group of three armored men standing around idly and occasionally giving the citizens a distrustful look.

The four of them stood there for an instant, staring at the bounty hunters, and one of the hunters swept his gaze over the crowd again, this time landing on Rynn and Kilderan.

They tried to turn away slowly, but the hunters were already trotting silently through the crowd towards them.

They all broke into a run, shoving aside the pedestrians and dodging a speeder.

"This way!" Yojackson shouted, turning a corner and leading them from the hunters.

All of the citizens stepped aside, looked on, or completely ignored the pursuit as the hooded strangers dashed down the street.

"Wait!" Kilderan yelled. "Follow me!" They merged with the newest wave of diverse outfits and appearances.

The group hurriedly turned a corner, and looking back they saw that the crowd had swallowed the hunters as well.

Panting, they came upon Thruhairth's market, which caused them to encounter an entirely new set of chaos.

A hovering cart filled with wrapped bundles hit a pothole in the road, nearly running over Rynn before Kilderan pulled him to the side.

Colorful booths lined the street for miles, and litter and pieces of lottery fliers and scraps of food and shredded flowers were strewn about the pathway. A tall, slender lady dressed in a gaudy white and gold outfit passed them with a frown making her long face less becoming. Rynn stepped out of her way. He noticed a man with a colorful cloak and a stringed instrument whose music was tying all the commotion together.

If he had felt overwhelmed at Port Illuvar, then he did not know what to call the feeling of standing amongst Thruhairth, that perfectly suited that fact that it was not only Arsteine's capital but the galaxy's capital.

They proceeded hastily wading through the crowd, but Rynn's gaze lingered on every booth they passed, as they were all so diverse and held no categorization: one with peculiar jewelry, another selling cuts of meat, and one weapons booth all stood side by side.

Rynn nearly tripped on his cloak. "Wait!"

They all turned abruptly, expecting danger.

"Kilderan, look!" Rynn rushed over to the weapons booth, where a beaten staff with a splintered end and several blades laid amongst other instruments just as uncommon. "It's my grandfather's staff!"

Kilderan came over to him and lifted the staff, examining it.

"How did it end up back here?"

"Those pirates must have lost it or sold it, or—" He looked at the vendor, a man with an eyepatch. "How much is this?"

He named the price, Yojackson tossed Kilderan the purse, and they paid for the staff. Rynn smiled, holding the staff proudly as he remembered Asold. But then he frowned. *He carried this because he knew someday he'd need to protect me. He...* Rynn looked over his shoulder at Kilderan, but quickly returned his gaze to the staff.

Kilderan bent to Rynn's ear. "Are you all right?"

"I miss him. I was always asking to go into the village, to go anywhere but the cottage. If I had known there was a reason—"

"It's not your fault that you—that you are the way you are." Kilderan cast a wary look at the vendor, who had ignored them and

89

was already bargaining with another customer. He placed a hand on Rynn's back, starting to lead him away. Rynn's veins pulsed.

However, they were interrupted by the parting of the crowd and a few shouts. They all looked up, confused, when a boy who seemed a few years older than Rynn came plowing into Kilderan.

Kilderan, caught unawares, glanced around at Aome, Rynn, and Yojackson. He placed his hands on the boy's shoulders and bent to his height. Kilderan's face disappeared behind the head of golden hair that glowed in the sunlight.

Rynn looked on, frowning. His veins flared up beneath his skin.

"Why are you running?" Kilderan asked the boy, but then Rynn saw an increasingly uncomfortable look come across Kilderan's features. Kilderan squinted and almost recoiled from the boy. The young man and the stranger stared at each other in silence for a moment before Kilderan resumed his full height and released the boy. "Just be careful, all right?"

The boy nodded, still not making a sound. He turned and stared at Aome and Rynn and Yojackson with two large bright blue eyes before darting away.

Rynn's veins fizzed and his fingers tingled. He sidled up to Kilderan's side. "What's going on?"

Kilderan merely shook his head, looking dazed and disoriented.

Yojackson gave Kilderan a questioning look that went unanswered before leading their party around another corner of the market.

XII

Kilderan still seemed distant even as they left the weapons booth and continued down the street at a speed that seemed only brisk and not suspicious.

Rynn glanced up at him a few times, preparing to speak, but he did not know what to say and he did not want to interrogate Kilderan. The encounter with the bounty hunters had left him wary and the young boy who had caused Kilderan to be so mystified made Rynn uneasy.

Yojackson expertly wove his way through the throng for a few more moments before Aome called out, "Yojackson! They've found us!"

Yojackson whipped around and then faced forward again, following Aome's finger to the dusty men in thin steel armor with weapons poised. The bounty hunters stood at the end of the street where there were no outlets.

Yojackson muttered, "Quickly. I see a way out."

They all fell into line and their cloaks made a blatant line of pitch black amongst the garish outfits that surrounded them.

"How far is it?" Aome asked.

"It's just the—" Yojackson turned and smirked. "Right here." He walked backwards for a few steps, palms spread.

Rynn stepped to the side and looked behind Yojackson to see a set of stairs leading below the city. He cocked his head and glanced at Kilderan.

"What?" Aome asked.

"The underground transport. They'll never find us there."

"Are you sure?" But even as he said that, Kilderan was skirting Aome and Yojackson and heading for the stairs with Rynn trailing behind him.

The bright light of day was rapidly blotted out by their descent into the lower level of the city. The noises of whirring machines and footsteps reverberated off of the walls.

"The transport's not here yet," Yojackson muttered, looking around at the few people who stood around idly, waiting for the underground transport to arrive. As he turned back towards his companions, however, there was a flood of citizens who raced down the stairs faster than the four had.

At the same instant, the transport pulled up beside them and its doors opened, hissing. The litter on the ground was trampled as everyone rushed on, some barely reaching the transport before it sped away again.

Rynn found himself uncomfortably wedged between two large merchants and surrounded on every side by everyone else in the crowd. He squeezed out of his spot and joined Kilderan at his side, close to the transport's emergency exit.

Looking over, he saw that the merchants had waded around inside the cramped train and were now crushing Aome and Yojackson against one another. The criminal reached his hand up and clenched one fist around the overhead stability grip as the train lurched forward.

Kilderan's head snapped up as a series of clicks sounded, and as he lowered his hand from his neck to his side, he glanced over Rynn to the other end of the transport. Rynn followed his gaze.

A group of men facing away from Rynn and Kilderan stood a few clusters of passengers away, their armor gleaming in a pallid way beneath the flickering green lighting of the train. Kilderan stooped to Rynn's ear. "I don't think they know where we are yet. They know we're here, obviously, but they're still looking for us."

Rynn looked up at him and nodded.

After a few seconds of trying to catch Yojackson's eye and waiting for him and Aome to untangle themselves, Kilderan managed to wave him over discreetly and point out the bounty hunters.

"What should we do?" Aome began to glance over her shoulder.

"Not that," Yojackson countered. "Don't let them see us." He slowly looked to Kilderan.

Kilderan glanced over his shoulder at the emergency exit, inhaling steadily. "I don't see any other way."

"We can't just open the emergency exit. Someone will notice." Aome adjusted her hood. "We need a distraction."

"Ah, no problem," Yojackson said. He turned and winked at them, saying, "Don't worry about me. I'll catch up." He smirked and raised an eyebrow.

"What—" Kilderan began.

Yojackson sauntered into the middle of the squashed passengers, readying himself before balling his hand into a fist and punching the portly merchant in his round, chubby face.

"Agh!" The man roared. "Now why'd you go and do that, you good-for-nothing—"

Yojackson allowed his hood to slide back, revealing his face to the entire car.

"Yojackson Owens!" one of the bounty hunters called.

"In the flesh. Though I must say, you—" He stumbled back as the merchant landed a blow to his face just as Yojackson had done.

Rynn's lips parted. He was about to say something when Yojackson quickly recovered and brought his fists up, the sea of passengers growing upset and chaotic.

"Okay, I'm opening the door," Kilderan announced in a whisper.

Slowly, silently, they slid the door at the end of the train open. There was a gust of wind as they did, and Rynn looked down at the blurred ground beneath them.

Kilderan held onto one of the stability grips and partially leaned out of the train. He turned back to Rynn and Aome. "There's a ladder on the side."

"I'll go first," Aome offered.

Kilderan gingerly gripped her waist as he helped to steady her as she climbed out of the train onto the side ladder. There was a clanging overhead, barely noticeable over the brawl Yojackson had started, as she reached the roof.

"Your turn." Kilderan turned to Rynn.

"What if I fall? And what about Yojackson?"

The wind whipped at his hair, pulling back his hood. "Yojackson can handle himself. He said he'll catch up to us, and he will. And I'll hold on to you, you won't fall." He attempted a small smile. "We've been in a few situations more deadly than this."

Rynn nodded as Kilderan's hands found his waist and he hoisted Rynn onto the ladder, almost falling out of the transport himself as he did so.

There was much more room on the roof of the underground transport than Rynn had expected, and he could completely stand without even nearing the ceiling. Kilderan brushed his dark hair aside even as the wind ruffled it again. He then heard a muffled cry from inside the train car.

"There are the others!"

Kilderan leaned out of the car and gazed up at Rynn, his blue eyes wild.

Aome appeared at Rynn's side and told Kilderan, "It's not too difficult. There's a small ledge to step up on to get to the ladder."

Kilderan nodded and lunged for the ladder, gripping it firmly even as his hair and cloak flailed behind him. He swung around and swiftly scrambled up the ladder. They all stood in unison once he was steadied.

Aome looked up at Kilderan, brow creased. "Yojackson? Is he coming?"

They all looked up, hearing gunshots below them.

"We need to jump!" Kilderan shouted.

"Are you insane? With your wounded leg?" Aome frowned at him.

"I'd be more insane to stay."

Dropping to their knees, Rynn, Kilderan, and Aome leaned over the edge of the roof. Yojackson leaned out of the transport's emergency door.

There was a cry, and another gunshot that shot out of the roof where Rynn was kneeling. Kilderan gestured for him to shift over.

"Get off the train and get to the temple! I'm fine!" A hand grabbed Yojackson's shoulder. Before disappearing from view, he called, "They're heading for the ladder!"

Aome and Rynn clutched at Kilderan's sleeves as he took a breath and then leapt from the speeding transport, landing in a heap on the ground below with Aome and Rynn on top of him.

Yojackson quickly faded from view as the train raced on, and the remaining three groaned and fell onto their backs.

After they had recovered, they scrambled to their feet.

"We can't just leave him behind!" Rynn exclaimed. "The bounty hunters know where he is now!"

"We need to get off of these tracks. More transports are bound to come through here," Kilderan said.

"Let's walk until we find the next stop," Aome suggested. "And then we have to find Yojackson."

"We need to get to Velle Deka. I don't want to waste any more time on Arsteine than we have to." Kilderan glanced at Rynn.

The tracks and the ceiling rumbled. A light dangling overhead flickered. They made their way to the edge of the magnetic tracks, Kilderan limping.

Aome pursed her lips. To Kilderan, she said, "Yojackson is as much a part of helping Rynn as you are. And now that you've told us you have the celestial blood too, we can't risk having either of you captured."

"I have to trust him. If he says we should go ahead without him, then we should. We can find Velle Deka quicker if we don't wait for him to catch up. Rynn is the main priority."

Aome sighed. "And Yojackson knew that." She frowned. "He's probably not even coming back from this, if we're being realistic." She dusted off her breeches. "All right. I'll take you to Kazari's temple."

Kilderan nodded his thanks. He winced.

"Kilderan?" Rynn crept up to his side.

"It's just my leg. I—"

"You probably shouldn't be walking on it so much. Come with me." Aome slid an arm around Kilderan, furrowing her brow as she supported his weight. "There has to be another set of stairs out of here. We'll just find someone to take us to the temple."

The rumbling in the tunnel grew louder, and Rynn paused in his tracks as the ground vibrated slightly beneath him. There was a glow approaching, but he found himself cemented to the ground. "Umm…" His lips parted.

The metallic nose of a transport appeared up ahead and in an instant Rynn found himself, eyes shut tight, shoved up against the wall of the tunnel, Kilderan pressing into him.

A gust of wind surrounded them and tugged at Kilderan's hair. Rynn opened his eyes, the train mere inches from him. Kilderan was the only thing separating them, and he stared into Rynn's wide eyes, his rapid breath warm on Rynn's skin.

Rynn's shoulder blades began to burn from having Asold's staff pressing into his back, but soon the train had passed.

Kilderan slowly backed away from him and brushed off Rynn's tunic. "Are you okay?"

"I think so." Rynn ruffled his already messed up hair. "Thanks…"

Kilderan adjusted his dark jacket.

"Let's hurry," Aome said. "The next stop can't be far now."

XIII

Yojackson ducked, the irritable merchant still trying to swing at him even as he rushed from the three bounty hunters at the back of the car to the door leading into the next section of the transport.

Hastily, he pulled the door open and squeezed through it.

The next car was less crowded, and more of the passengers were seated. He frowned and looked straight ahead at the door standing before him—the door to the control room. The train was moving very quickly, however, and he had no idea how far he had gone from his companions or where he would end up in such a large capital city.

There was more shouting coming from the car behind him.

First I need to deal with those blasted bounty hunters. He reached for his pistol, and, pulling it from the holster, returned to the door.

Yojackson cracked the portal open very slightly, enough for his gun to fit through, and squinted.

Being so close to Yojackson, his gun was deafeningly loud, but one of the hunters fell back. "One down," he muttered. Then louder, he called, "Come and get me, boys!"

He whirled around and dashed for the control room. The door did not open for him, and he tried to pull it back several times before resorting to pounding on it and once even kicking it. A slot in the door slid back and the dull brown eyes of the engineer appeared in its place.

"Let me in!"

"Why would I do that? You're not authorized," the man spat in an annoyed voice.

Yojackson swore. "Just open the door, blast it!" He bit his lip and thought for a moment, and then a smirk broke across his face. He held his pistol directly in front of the man's narrowed eyes.

"Ah!" The man recoiled. He disappeared, but the door made a clanging noise and Yojackson could tell his back was against the door. "Now, sir, kindly put that thing down," he drawled. "Why do you even want in here?"

"To stop this blasted transport." Yojackson did not lower his pistol. "I don't have time for this." He slid the gun into the open slot and fired it. "Open up or next time it's your head!"

A few moments later, the door opened and the fearful man stood in the corner of the room, his hands shielding his face. "Don't hurt me, sir. I've got nothing to do with this…this… whatever you're doing."

Yojackson muttered something under his breath and went over to the man. "Stop the transport now."

"We'll hold up the tunnel!"

Yojackson held up the pistol.

The man sighed, clearly irritated although he was frightened. He moved to the controls and after pulling a few levers the train screeched on the tracks and slowly came to a halt.

Yojackson turned and deserted him, but as he turned around he looked upon the two remaining bounty hunters with their weapons in hand.

"Fancy meeting you here. Excuse me, I'll just be on my way, now."

One of them aimed their gun at Yojackson. "This is the largest payment I've ever seen on any bounty in my entire life. You're coming with us."

Yojackson smirked. "Emperor Dusek flatters me. But I've got somewhere I need to be." He pulled his second pistol out of his other holster and shot at them, rushing between them immediately after doing so.

He wasted no time in departing the transport, leaping down onto the tracks, holstering the pistols, and breaking into a run and never looking over his shoulder.

•••

Soon, when he was exhausted from running, he slowed, catching his breath. He glanced around and noticed a light not too far away. Panting, he made his way toward it.

Gradually, the sound of a crowd reached his ears and he perked up slightly, expecting to have found a set of stairs leading to Thruhairth's streets.

As he neared it, though, he realized that it was indeed a set of stairs, but one that led even further underground.

The muffled voices cried out again and he quickly made his way down the grimy steps into another tunnel that was crumbling and covered in stains and unintelligible graffiti. Following the glow that pulsed around the corner, Yojackson stumbled upon a dark, torn curtain hung across the large tunnel. The greenish glow tried to escape from behind it.

Yojackson squinted at the curtain and without a moment of hesitation pulled it back and stepped inside.

The beat of some strange music reached his ears and a dozen women in glittering if revealing dresses glanced his way before being summoned to the sides of even more questionable men. There was a flickering light overhead casting either a blue or green glow around the tunnel. The room was heavy with colored tendrils of odorous smoke. As Yojackson slowly walked through the tunnel and examined the people there, he came upon a polished, shining racing cycle sitting amongst the filth and murky puddles inside the tunnel.

He raised his eyebrows and whistled. "Well. Wonder what such a nice vehicle is doing in a place this," he muttered to himself.

A woman with green skin slid up to his side and locked arms with him. "Admiring Gourlin's cycle?"

"So this one's taken, huh?"

She tossed her dark hair. "Gourlin might be willing to sell it to such a handsome man like yourself."

Yojackson furrowed his brow. "Where is he?"

She stepped away from him and adjusted the strap of her dress. Waving her hand idly, she said, "Around." She chuckled before gliding away.

Yojackson scratched his chin before continuing on his way. *A cycle like that would reunite me with Kip and the others in no time.*

After avoiding more flamboyant women, Yojackson encountered an odd arrangement of tables with around five people seated at each. A gaunt man stepped towards him.

"These games are about over. Join in the next round."

Yojackson waved away the smoke of the man's cigar and leaned against the wall, smoothing his jacket. A gnarled rat ran past his ankle.

"Have a drink while you wait," the scrawny man said, holding out a tray of cracked glasses filled with a queer pink liquid.

Yojackson shrugged and took two of the small glasses and raised them to the man in thanks, smirking.

• • •

He had been waiting around for what seemed like hours when finally someone called out, "Open tables!"

Yojackson's head snapped up and he stepped in front of the line that was forming in front of the scrawny man. There were a few shouts of protest, but he kept walking. He bumped one of the tables as a short man with tufted ears was arranging a jumbled collection of cards and hologram devices. The man squawked at him.

The tables began to fill, and Yojackson was certain he had not seen the Gourlin man who owned the cycle.

"Hey, friend! Take a seat!"

He spun around to see a large, pudgy creature wearing a poorly-fitting violet jacket and smoking a long glass pipe and waving a meaty hand at him. In actuality, he looked more like an overgrown toad than any kind of man.

Yojackson frowned at him for an instant, before asking, "What are we playing?"

He leaned back and rested his folded hands on his large stomach. "Just a quick game of Rue." He chuckled. "Take a seat. One of my regulars can sit this one out."

Yojackson listed his head, eyeing the large pouch of something glittering sitting next to the frog man. "Don't mind if I do. Rue happens to be one of my favorite games."

The creature spread his palms as more patrons joined the table and a few women, including the green-skinned one Yojackson had encountered earlier, leaned on the table with long, thin cigars between their fingers that emitted yellow smoke.

A tall man sitting hunched over next to the frog creature glanced, almost glared, at Yojackson.

Yojackson seated himself at the table across from the frog man, who chuckled in delight.

"Yini, hand the man a cigar."

Yojackson frowned at the small tufted-eared man who had screeched at him earlier as a fat cigar was slid into his waiting palm. As he lit the cigar, he stared absently at the frog man, apparently the head of the table.

"What's your name, anyway, friend?"

Yojackson lowered his gaze to the hologram device being slid across the table to him. Mumbling with the cigar in his mouth, he quickly invented an alias. "It's Benson."

The green-skinned woman leaned close to the toad. "I haven't seen his face around here before."

"Yeah," the frog croaked. "Yeah! What are you doing here, friend? How'd you find this place, anyways?"

Yojackson smiled. "I received some inside information from a friend. And as for why I'm here, I'm looking for a man called Gourlin. He's got a pretty slick cycle I was checking out earlier."

The frog coughed on his pipe and shared a knowing look with the table. "Well, Benson...you've found your chap."

Yojackson sat forward, brow creased. "*You're* Gourlin?"

The toad laughed, revealing two flapping tongues. "That I am." He suddenly sat up and raised a fist. "Change the music, blast you! Something that I like!" He quickly returned his attention to Yojackson, wiggling his pipe back into position. "And you are interested in my racing cycle, eh?" He did not wait for Yojackson to reply before delving into an explanation. "I have many others, and I may be willing to wager it in this game at some point, just to humor you—I never lose at Rue!" Everyone around the table, save Yojackson, shared in a round of raspy laughter.

Yojackson leaned on his elbows, fiddling with the hologram device before switching it on to display a screen listing the table's wagers. He smirked. "Fine. And I'll take that pouch of credits, too."

"Woah, now, friend." He turned to the two men and one woman sitting on his side of the table. "He's a confident one." He squinted at Yojackson. "That's quite a bet. Do you even have anything to put up?"

"Does he even have enough money for the entry fee?" asked one man, eliciting more chuckling.

A man carrying a tray of small half-cooked reptiles—some still wriggling—came up to their table and offered Gourlin one of the fattest frogs, which the toad readily took and scarfed down sloppily.

"I have money," Yojackson promised. Reaching into his coat pocket, he produced a fistful of jewelry and set it on the table: a pair of pearl earrings and a matching pearl and gold necklace, a brooch of the emperor's insignia, and then he pulled two diamond rings from his own fingers. "I got these directly from the palace."

Gourlin laughed and showed his slimy tongues again. "You expect me to believe that, friend? Where's your proof?"

"I don't need proof. If you always win, why even bother?"

The toad scratched his chin, contemplating. "Fine. Pay your fees, everyone."

Yojackson readily paid the hologram half of all of the credits in the pouch he had stolen from the bounty hunter on Ganymede.

"And, deal!" declared the scrawny man.

Yojackson sat back and sighed, carefully watching Gourlin as he dealt the cards. Smoke filled the atmosphere and everyone at the table continued to add to the already heavy air.

Yojackson received his cards and drew them to himself, making certain there was no chance anyone could tell the signs.

"Anyone backing out now?" asked the man.

No one did, and affirmed their wagers.

"Dice!" called the man.

Gourlin rolled the five golden dice in his slimy hand and then let them roll onto the table. "Aha!" yelled the toad. "The signs are in my favor!" He laid his cards for all of them to see. All but one of them matched perfectly with the dice.

Yojackson's mouth fell open and he looked from the dice to his own cards, feigning surprise. "Oh, but now *you* are too confident." He made a show of laying his cards down before them, with every one matching the dice.

The toad raised what seemed like his eyebrows. "Beginner's luck," he muttered.

"That's where you're wrong, *friend*," Yojackson said, scooping up the pouches of credits and his jewelry towards him. "I am no beginner."

"Scum," Gourlin mumbled. But suddenly he threw his hands in the air, laughing lightheartedly. "Another game! You'll see you are mistaken."

"Very well. I have all the time in the world."

"Fresh cards!" The scrawny man reluctantly handed Yojackson a new pile.

"What do you wager this time, friend?" Gourlin ran one of his tongues over his bloated lips.

Yojackson shoved his prize back into the middle of the table. "Double or nothing."

Gourlin glanced around, his throat bulging as he breathed. He smiled, not one of his appealing features, if he even had any. "All right. Dice!" He rolled the golden cubes onto the table.

Yojackson scanned the signs and then chuckled to himself as Gourlin scowled at him and the scrawny man frowned. "Matching cards," Yojackson said. He shrugged. "Beginner's luck."

"You're cheating, somehow," insisted Gourlin.

"I told you, Rue is one of my favorite games. I guess I just have that special luck." Yojackson waved a hand around idly.

After thinking for a moment, Gourlin said, "Another game, then. You will learn your lesson, Benson."

•••

"And…more matches than anyone at this table." Yojackson smiled.

"This is ridiculous!" cried one of the men. "Gourlin, walk away before this scoundrel cleans us all out!"

"Don't be stubborn!" begged another.

"I am the head of this table, and you should consider yourself lucky to have the privilege of playing with me, friends." Gourlin glared at all of them. "Or do you need a reminder?"

They remained silent.

"Well, friend, you are not very smart to keep winning against me, you know that?"

"I'm smart enough to know I'm not your *friend*," Yojackson retorted. "And if I didn't know any better I'd say you're intimidated by me."

Gourlin moved to stand, growling at Yojackson. The green-skinned woman stepped in. "Look how many people have gathered to watch, Gourlin. You started this outfit for entertainment, and that's exactly what you're giving them."

As the frog settled down, she winked flirtatiously at Yojackson.

"She's right," Yojackson said. "One more game and I'll leave you to your…entertainment." He leaned across the table and muttered, "I promise I'll bend just this once, to keep up the suspense."

"You apparently know your way around the criminal world. You should know a promise means absolutely nothing around here."

"I'm teasing. You should've known that." Yojackson flashed his smile, propping his feet up on the table.

Gourlin glared at him and said, gritting his teeth, "And I would love to, friend, but as you can see I have hardly anything left to bet."

Yojackson bit his lip, pretending to think. His eyes suddenly widened. "How about that cycle?"

"That's my best racer!"

"Come on, Gourlin. All of this loot could come right back to you. Just one last game. You know you want to."

The toad sat for a moment, tapping his finger on the table to the music. "Fine. The cycle, for everything you've basically stolen from me."

"Fine," Yojackson echoed.

"We're backing out, though, Gourlin," one of the players said, to which the frog waved his hand carelessly.

"Deal!" The cards were laid down.

Gourlin peered at his cards, and Yojackson briefly scanned his own.

Gourlin rolled the handful of dice.

Yojackson sat forward before falling back and sighing, cursing under his breath.

"All matches but one," the gaunt man said of Gourlin's cards.

"What did I say? I always win at Rue!" This was followed by loud cheers.

Yojackson began to shake his head. *Now you've really done it.* "Ah! Wait!" He quickly flipped his card over. He laughed. "It was upside down. My mistake. Looks like I've got one more match than you, toad. Which would make me, what? The winner?"

The cheers were silenced.

Gourlin gaped at Yojackson's cards. "How—"

Yojackson swept all of the jewelry and coin purses to his side of the table. "I'll just be heading for that cycle."

"You must have cheated! You must have!" Gourlin stood and pointed a slime-covered finger at Yojackson. He swore several times, walking away. As he did so, he yelled, "What did I say about that blasted music!"

After emptying his tall glass of green, fizzing liquid at the table, Yojackson took his prize in his arms and carefully carried it all through the old tunnel to the polished racing cycle nearer to the entrance.

Yojackson guided the cycle out of the hidden gambling den, up the steps, and into the main tunnel before jumping into it, admiring the pouches of money and jewelry that sat behind him.

"Hold it right there, Benson!"

Yojackson's head whipped around to see two tall but thin men slinking towards him. He sighed and dismounted the cycle, listing his head.

"You can't cheat against the boss and get away with it," one of the men told him.

Yojackson scanned their shabby outfits and empty holsters and sheaths.

"I just did," Yojackson said, smirking and preparing to turn back to the cycle.

A hand came up and grasped his shoulder, jerking him around to face its owner.

Yojackson quickly brought up a fist and punched the man before shoving him down.

The fallen gambler's companion rushed towards the pirate and began to tackle him, but Yojackson elbowed the man's stomach multiple times before throwing the man onto the ground.

By that time, the previously stunned man was standing back up and holding balled fists up, glowering at Yojackson.

Yojackson reached for his pistol and aimed it at the men. "I didn't cheat," he asserted. "So—"

Before he could finish, the men were already backing away and merging with the slime-covered wall.

Yojackson returned to the cycle and mounted it with an air of satisfaction.

He pressed the communications switch and was answered by a static voice whose words he could barely make out, though he could understand them enough to reply, "Yeah…I just located an illegal gambling club below the main transport tunnels. Some pretty shady characters, too. They seem dangerous, yes, and I definitely think you should…*apprehend* them." The communication chirped and was silent, and Yojackson smirked at the rumble of the cycle beneath him as he sped out of the tunnels onto the streets of the city.

XIV

"Where did you say you needed taken to?" asked the middle-aged woman who sat at a booth counting credits.

"Kazari's temple," Aome replied. "It isn't too far out of the city, is it?"

"Lady, have you never been to Thruhairth? It's a maze that goes on for hours if you don't know the right streets to head down. And even if I wanted to escort you, my last speeder left around an hour ago."

"We could pay you double," Kilderan interjected.

Aome leaned over to him. "We don't have any money, remember?"

Rynn turned away from them and gazed past the buildings and booths to the barely visible palace that loomed over everything. He wondered if the emperor knew where they were at that very moment. He also wondered if he really was being tracked. He stretched his arms out, trying to escape the long sleeves of his oversized tunic.

"Let's try somewhere else," Aome muttered.

"Let's go, Rynn," Kilderan said.

They left the booth and stepped back out into the crowded street.

"Are we going to make it to the temple?" Rynn asked, someone brushing against his shoulder.

"Not today, not if we can't find someone willing to take us so far out of Thruhairth," Kilderan explained.

"What about Yojackson? Do you think he'll make it back?"

Aome scoffed. "Do you believe he's even making an effort? If he's the planet-hopping freebooter that I think he is, he left us behind as soon as we jumped off of that transport."

Kilderan frowned at her. "I trust him. I don't believe he's as careless as you think he is."

"He's a pirate, Kilderan. His life has probably consisted of nothing but shooting those pistols and hanging out at taverns. He wouldn't help a child and his brother, and a priestess, would he?"

"You're assuming too much. I knew Yojackson when I was a child, and I saved his life." Kilderan shrugged. "He hasn't forgotten it, and even went out of his way to make certain I knew that."

"Oh." Aome furrowed her brow and held a hand on her forehead. "I'm sorry. He's your friend." She raised an eyebrow. "But my opinion won't change."

Kilderan gave her a skeptical look, at which she said, "It won't."

Rynn glanced at Kilderan. "Look at the sky. It's getting darker."

He nodded. "I shouldn't be walking so much on my injured leg, either. We need to find a means of reaching the temple, and quickly."

• • •

They wandered down the streets, eventually ending back up at the market by the time the suns were setting. The booths were empty, and some nonpermanent ones were even missing causing wide gaps in the shopping district. Even more litter than had been there before was now blown around by the wind. Through the spaces in the buildings, an orange light shone onto the street.

Rynn glanced around, the street that had once been so busy now eerie in its vacancy. They passed a few of the merchants who were carrying packs away, and then Rynn saw a man at one booth loading crates into a large cart. "What about that?" he asked Kilderan, pointing. "Could that take us to the temple?"

"If the man will let us ride with him." He turned and they followed him over to the cart. "Where is this cart headed?"

The man looked up. "Huh?"

"Will you be driving this cart to the outskirts?"

He thought for a moment. "Yes…"

"We don't mean to trouble you, but will you let us ride with you?" Kilderan asked. "There aren't any transports available, and—"

"Yeah, yeah. I'm not associating with a bunch of strangers."

"We won't—"

"Wait..." Holding a hand up, he looked past Kilderan to Aome. "Are you a priestess at Kazari's temple?"

She frowned. "How could you tell?"

He lowered his gaze, a solemn shadow coming over his face. He gestured at her wrist. "The beads. My sister was one of the older priestesses there, that's how I know. I'll take you to the outskirts. I'll help you reach the temple."

Aome shoved in front of Kilderan. "Thank you so much."

He nodded to her and stepped aside to let them into the metal cart, but not before he shoved the crates aside and laid a cloth down for Aome to sit on. He mounted the small speeder that was towing the cart and it soon sputtered to life and they left the street behind.

•••

The capital city had grown quiet with the dispersing of the merchants, but Rynn did not realize the constant, inescapable humming was gone from his ears until the silence of the barely-visited outskirts took its place. Everything around him was dark, as the cart was, he guessed, likely the slowest transportation available in the city. He could hardly make out the pitch-black shapes of Kilderan and Aome beside him.

He drew his knees to his chest and rested his chin there, the only light excessively dim lanterns scattered on either side of the street.

Kilderan's voice so close to his ear caused Rynn to jump. "How far until we are out of the city?"

The black shape of the driver turned towards them, and Rynn only knew this because the silhouette shifted. "Not too far, but not until dawn. But night is almost over."

"Can't you drive a little quicker?" Kilderan asked. "We've stayed in the city for too long."

"The speeder's engine has been on the fritz for a while, and I don't wanna push it."

With that, Kilderan reclined against the metal wall and sighed.

Rynn leaned over to him and whispered, "Are we gonna be discovered?" The cart met a dip in the road, and he held onto his staff to be certain it would not fall out of his grip and injure someone.

"If they're tracking the ship, then they wouldn't know where we are."

"And if they aren't?" Aome put in.

She went unanswered, for the cart stopped suddenly and its owner perked up

"What's going on?" Aome asked.

"Blast!" the man exclaimed. "The engine died." He slid out of the speeder and came around the side of the cart to speak with them. "Sorry folks. Looks like this is as far as I can take you."

Rynn and the others reluctantly left the cart.

"Thank you anyway," Aome said. "Kazari's temple will appreciate it."

He did not answer her and immediately turned away, examining the engine.

Looking at Rynn and Kilderan, Aome shrugged.

"Let's go," Kilderan said.

At that, they began to plod down the street, Kilderan limping slightly. In those few moments the suns had begun to emerge from behind the horizon, casting a still dark but helpful lavender glow on everything.

・・・

When they finally neared the end of the outskirts, the suns were about to reach their zenith and the street stretched out in front of them into a less maintained road. The crowds had emerged once more, but Rynn found himself growing more and more peaceful the further the city—the palace—became.

He turned to Kilderan, about to speak, when the young man himself stopped suddenly and asked Aome, "How far do you think the temple is?"

She thought for a moment, glancing around at their surroundings. "Kazari's temple isn't too far outside the city, but at the rate we're going—"

"I don't want us to walk all that way," Kilderan interrupted, his tone anxious. "Technically, we're still in the city. It makes me uncomfortable." He looked at Rynn.

The clamor of the city spilled into the outskirts and an unusually loud speeder engine roared in the distance.

"Kilderan?" Rynn blinked away the blinding late morning sun. "What about Yojackson? Is he coming back?"

"He's going to be fine. I'm trying to keep *you* safe, though."

Aome placed her hands on her hips. "I really don't think he's coming back. And good riddance. I'd had enough of that presumptuous smirking and brash spirit."

The speeder engine grew closer.

Aome turned to Kilderan and Rynn, about to continue, when they all heard, "Why, sounds like you missed me, priestess!"

Aome's mouth fell open and she spun around.

Yojackson appeared on a polished orange cycle that looked unusually new. A large pouch sat behind him.

"Jack?" Kilderan smiled. "You're alive!"

Yojackson cocked an eyebrow. "Of course I'm alive!"

"I thought you were never gonna make it back!" Rynn exclaimed.

Aome crossed her arms. "You could have at least stolen a cycle that looks like it belongs to you."

Yojackson halted the cycle and sauntered up to her. "It *does* belong to me, priestess. It's our ticket out of this obnoxious city." He smirked.

Aome recoiled, disbelief etched across her features. "How…"

He waved a hand. "It's a long story." He glanced at Kilderan and Rynn. "And we have a temple to get to."

Kilderan and Rynn shared a surprised smile.

The pirate turned back to the cycle and walked towards it. "It's a tight squeeze, but it'll get us there faster than walking."

They made their way to the racing vehicle and Kilderan helped Rynn onto it, though Aome refused assistance.

Their bodies pressed into one another and Aome was forced to wrap her arms around Yojackson's waist. Then she said to him, "I warrant that story isn't *too* long."

He shrugged. "Ah, it would bore you anyway."

XV

The cycle vibrated beneath Rynn's legs and he tightened his arms around Kilderan's waist. He craned his neck to ask Yojackson, "How far to the temple?"

The man looked towards Aome.

She turned back to Rynn. "Very, very close. I remember these roads."

"We're almost one step closer to getting you away from this place," Kilderan told Rynn. To Aome, he said, "Are you sure Velle Deka really knows where the celestial spring is?"

"She is very wise, and taught me everything I know. In fact, she was still in the process of sharing her knowledge of the goddesses and the stars with me when I left for my trip. I wouldn't have taken you all this way if I wasn't certain she had the information you need," she assured him.

Compared to walking, Rynn found that the cycle brought them away from the outskirts and into the small stretch of land free from civilization exceptionally quickly.

When he gazed up at the sky, the suns seemed to be in the same position as when Yojackson first arrived. Kilderan continually disrupted Rynn's position on the cycle with his constant fidgeting and glancing behind them. His hair blew in the wind created by the cycle and into Rynn's face, the hasty braid on one side of his head coming undone.

Rynn looked at the landscape that Aome said was so familiar, and thought about what Kilderan had told him. *We're almost one step closer to getting you away from this place. This place. Arsteine? The galaxy? The mortal realm?* A small ribbon of fear curled around his mind as he considered what Kilderan was really doing for him, what would actually happen to him. It then occurred to him that he did not know anything except that it would mean leaving behind mortality and the world that he had not really gotten to live in anyway. He frowned, troubled and confused.

"Over the hill," Aome told Yojackson. "Yojackson, stop the cycle!"

He obeyed, and the abrupt stop very nearly flung them all off of the vehicle. "What's wrong?" he asked.

"Sorry," she said, laughing. "We almost sped right past it. Follow me."

She did not waste time waiting for the others to dismount, and by the time they had she was already standing on the crest of the hill.

The others joined her and looked out across the dip in the land at a meadow of delicate white flowers that rose to their waists as they started down the hill and spread legions of small petals with every bout of wind that rustled them. Trees stood like tall, verdant spires set on fire by the three setting suns. They bowed their tops in a solemn way, as if to mourn the passing of something only they knew of. Save for the gentle breeze disturbing the travelers' hair, the air was calm and warm, like a caress.

It seemed so far from Thruhairth everywhere Rynn looked, and the presence of peace and a feeling like he could lie in the lea of florets under the wispy late morning clouds for the rest of his immortal existence overtook him.

"The temple is just around the clump of trees up there," Aome said, gesturing. She smiled and looked down at her clothes. "Mother Deka would not really approve of this, I think." But then she shrugged.

"Why does it feel like it took us a week to get from the city to the temple?" Yojackson asked. "It can't be *that* far from the city..."

"It isn't," Aome said. "It's just far enough so that everyone who is so opposed to the goddesses and their followers can't reach it so easily."

Yojackson cocked an eyebrow at her.

Kilderan came up behind Rynn. "We're here, Rynn," he whispered. "This priestess can tell us where the spring is."

Rynn nodded silently, gazing out at the treetops. "But what is that?"

Every pair of eyes followed his gesture.

Aome gasped. She stared at the gray tendrils of smoke curling around in the air above the tips of the trees for one instant more before breaking into a run.

Rynn, Kilderan, and Yojackson joined her, puzzled.

113

They all raced across the serene field, though Kilderan was a little slower than Rynn and Yojackson due to his limp, disrupting the white flowers and snapping their stems and shaking their petals off. A haze of pollen hung in the air. Aome ran unusually fast, a rush in her gait that was absent from the three others.

Soon they came to the copse of trees where Kazari's temple stood. But then Rynn saw it.

The temple was in complete ruin, with amber-colored flames licking its sides and the surrounding trees. There were a few pitch black spots on the white walls, and linens and flowerpots and tomes, all covered in ash, were scattered in the grass.

"Mother Deka!" Aome called, running towards the crumbling temple. "Is there anyone here?" She turned and then another gasp came from her. The white-clad bodies of priestesses were lying face down in the meadow flowers. She approached them and studied their cinder- and blood-stained robes. "Mother Deka!" she screamed again, her voice becoming choked. "Is there anybody here?"

Part of the burning temple crashed down and there was a shout from inside it. Aome turned to Rynn, Kilderan, and Yojackson with tears welling in her eyes. She began to shake her head before darting into the temple.

"Aome!" Yojackson called.

A gust of wind blew the smoke into their faces and they all coughed, eyes watering. Rynn rubbed his eyes and realized it was not only the smoke causing his tears. Kilderan pulled him against his chest in a slack embrace, obscuring the boy's vision.

After a few long moments, Yojackson glanced at Kilderan. "She hasn't come out. What the—"

"Aome!" Kilderan shouted.

The priestess emerged from the burning building, covered in dark ash, with a woman in white leaning on her.

She staggered towards them and then let the woman go, slumping to the ground and staring at her temple collapse. Yojackson and the others stepped towards her.

"They were my family. That was my home," she murmured, barely audible over the flames. She began to attend to the woman, who had a large wound on her temple that was caked with gore. "Are you all right?"

The woman's lips parted, and she coughed, a stream of blood running out of the side of her mouth. "The emperor…" She coughed again. "…ordered to destroy every temple and…" A cough. "…and monument honoring the goddesses. They burned it."

Aome's brow creased and she clutched the shoulders of the priestess. "And the high priestess? Mother Deka?" She sniffed.

The woman began to choke and after the fit ceased, she responded, "She…she…" She cast her eyes toward the blue sky, so oblivious to the tragedy unfolding beneath its cheerful wings. "She escaped."

Aome sighed in relief.

The woman's words became rushed and slurred. "She's fled beneath the city, where she is hiding. But they are looking for her. At the palace. They want to kill her. She's one of the only remaining maidservants." Here the priestess turned away from Aome and to the sky again, her face pallid and smeared with ash. "The stars…" she whispered. "Sister, do you see them? They are growing closer. I think…" Her eyes then grew blank but a small smile ghosted her lips and she sighed. An unsettling tranquility came over her features.

Aome smoothed the woman's white robe and closed her eyelids. She rubbed her own eyes, then, and wiped her face with the sleeve of her now-tattered leather jacket. She took another look at the temple and then doubled over, sobbing.

Rynn glanced at Kilderan, concern and fear and sadness engulfing him. To see Aome so overwhelmed made him uncertain of if he should join her or back away into his brother's arms again. He looked at Kazari's burning temple. He recalled his own mother's name. *Zelia. It wasn't her temple.* He blinked. *But it was her sister's. It was her sister's memory. My aunt.* He sniffed and began to hiccup, distressed by Aome and the destroyed shrine but also remembering his grandfather, who had been murdered by the emperor's orders as well. He turned and embraced Kilderan, coughing. "They burned it. They killed them all," he bawled.

Kilderan's lips were pressed into a firm line, and he stared absently at the scarlet-tipped flames. When Rynn looked up at him, his eyes were filled with a fear that scared Rynn, though it was hardly noticeable beneath a regretful, sorrowful look that represented in a mist of tears over his cold, pale blue eyes.

• • •

The stillness of the meadow did not change at all with the coming of dusk, it only took on a fiery tint much like Kazari's temple that shone through the trees and into their faces.

Rynn watched as Yojackson assisted Aome in burying every corpse that they had found at the shrine. He stood and glanced at Kilderan, who was facing the setting suns, but then turned back to Aome. Rynn stared at the disturbed soil that now covered the bodies, forming distinct humps in the ground. Bunches of the white flowers that graced the field were scattered over the burials.

Aome hung her head. "I didn't know all of them, but I knew most of them."

Rynn could tell that Yojackson wanted to say something, but could not formulate something that was tender and sympathetic enough. Rynn stepped gingerly across the grass to stand by Aome's side.

She looked down at him, eyes still glistening. She held a white flower limply in her hand.

He gazed up into her emerald green eyes, a tear falling from the corner of his own eye. He thought of Asold.

The noise of Aome's voice sounded alien after such pensive silence. "Will you bless them?"

Rynn frowned. "What?"

"Will you give your blessing to my departed sisters, as a celestial child? It would mean very much to me, and—and to them."

Rynn, not fully comprehending the reverence she placed in him, nodded. "Umm…" He looked at the mounds. The trees swayed. "…Safe passage to wherever you are going. You—you carry my blessing." He felt odd saying the words, because he did not understand what exactly he should have said or what it meant for the deceased priestesses. He wondered if the goddesses could hear him.

He glanced warily at Aome, who nodded her approval and handed him the white blossom, which he laid on one of the mounds, that of the wounded priestess Aome had retrieved from the temple. They stood wordlessly for a few more moments, and Yojackson joined them, though he kept glancing over at Kilderan.

Finally Aome stepped away. "We should leave," she muttered.

"Come here," Kilderan said to them. Once they had, he gestured to the other side of the meadow, where a small hill rose. "Do you see that?"

Rynn squinted into the light of the suns, his eyes watering, but he could make out the silhouette of some sort of cart.

Another silhouette emerged from the first, and they saw that it was a man. The figure, noticing them, raised an arm in what looked like greeting.

"Should we head for the cycle?" Yojackson asked.

"Maybe," Kilderan said. He withdrew from his daze. "Yes."

They all turned in unison and slowly walked through the meadow and to the hill where Yojackson's shining racing vehicle sat gleaming in the sunset.

By the time they reached the cycle and Yojackson began to drive it through the meadow, the cart and the man were already halfway to them.

"Hey!" the man called.

The speeder halted, though none of them dismounted. A few feet separated them and the man, who climbed down from his own small, rusty vehicle and approached them. He was elderly, and wearing a dusty hat, loose trousers, a tunic, and a belt with a holstered pistol. "Are you folks lost?"

It was a moment before finally Kilderan answered, "We're travelers. We came for the temple, but—"

"Yes." The man took off his hat. "We heard them coming, but thought it would be better to hide and stay out of trouble. The emperor doesn't really know we're out here."

"What do you mean?" Kilderan asked.

The man turned back to the speeder and the cart and said, "I have a small farm not too far from here, but no one ever comes out this way, especially not to see the temple." He brushed his hands together. "Look, folks, I really am sorry about the temple. Was anyone hurt?"

Aome told him, "They were all killed."

Surprise came across his face. "There have been rumors for a while that the emperor intended to do something about the fact that the goddesses and their creed were still so prominent. But destroying what was the largest temple…I wonder what prompted him to do it now."

Kilderan stared at the ground, and Aome gazed up at the sky.

"Well, I'll let you be on your way." He gave them a friendly smile, placing his hat back on his head.

"We have nowhere to go. The temple was our destination." Kilderan pulled the sleeves of his tunic down.

"Why don't you stay with us for a while? You all look tired and hungry. We have food and an extra room."

"I don't know—" Kilderan started.

Aome interrupted. "Thank you. That would be exactly what we need." She glanced back at Kilderan and whispered, "This *is* what we need. It's far from the city, but close enough to it that we can find Velle Deka after we regroup."

He did not answer her, and Rynn shifted behind him, suddenly starving now that the man had mentioned food.

"It's not too far," the man explained. "You can follow behind on that fancy cycle of yours."

Aome nodded to Yojackson and they steadily made their way across the field, the sky changing from orange and gold to lavender. Rynn looked over his shoulder before brushing his hair out of his eyes and facing forward to the line of trees where he felt they would be safe, at least for the moment.

XVI

The farm was in an open area with trees at its back and the sky hanging overhead like a smooth inky sheet slowly being punctured by the pinpoints of light that were the stars. The farm consisted of a modest, ivy-covered building from inside which came a golden light and a small patch of tilled soil where vegetables were halfway done growing. The peaceful evening was disrupted by the growl of the two speeders as they made their way up to the quaint, overgrown house.

The man parked his speeder and cart near a small shed, but Yojackson stopped his own vehicle on the dusty path leading to the house. He, Rynn, Kilderan, and Aome then piled on one another in an effort to get out of the tight seating arrangement.

The owner of the farm came over to them and held a hand out to Yojackson. "My name is Koto, by the way."

"Yo—" He swiftly turned back to Kilderan and the others. "Jack. My name is Jack." He smiled uneasily.

Koto smiled and heartily shook his hand. "I take it you're the head of this group?"

Yojackson smirked. "Ha. Indeed I am." He placed his hands on his hips proudly, though Aome squinted at him.

Koto then looked past Yojackson to the others. "And you all are?"

"My name is Aome."

Koto tipped his hat.

"Kilderan."

Rynn accepted the hand held out to him and said, "Rynn."

"Nice to meet you, young man." Koto clapped his hands together. "Won't you come inside? My wife should know that we have visitors."

They followed him into the house and suddenly a warm gust of air hit Rynn's face, as well as a fragrance of spices and wood. The woods and meadow had taken on a cold, gloomy blue tint, thus making the cottage seem golden and even warmer and more inviting. The cottage was larger than Rynn's home, and on one side was a window with a table beneath it holding a hologram displayer and an empty but food-stained bowl. There were two ancient-looking chairs situated nearby. On the other side was a small kitchen where a woman stood at the sink. A dark hallway ran through the middle of the two sides.

"Iva, I found these travelers out in the meadow near Kazari's temple."

The woman turned around. She had mousy hair that despite the wrinkles on her face had not turned gray yet and a bright green dress with large, billowy sleeves. She gave them a small smile. "The temple?" she asked her husband.

He shook his head and she lowered her gaze.

"Did you ever visit the temple?" Aome asked her.

She nodded. "We know that a lot of people were and are strongly opposed to the goddesses and their memory, including the emperor. But we feel that they should be honored. To see the temple destroyed…"

It was a moment before Aome said, "I was a priestess there."

Iva's eyes lit up. "Really? Oh, that's wonderful! We are so honored, Sister."

Aome dipped her head.

"I invited them to stay with us for a while, until they have to leave," Koto explained. He placed his hat on the table and unfastened the belt holding his gun.

Iva nodded vigorously and smiled. "Of course! I have a meal that will be ready in a short while, but it would give you all enough time to bathe." She hastily looked them all over. "I think I have some extra clothes in the bedroom just inside that door."

"Thank you," Aome said.

In a line, the four of them followed Iva down the hall and to a small room.

"And there's a room that you could all stay in for the night, too." She glanced between Kilderan and Yojackson, who both towered over her.

Aome folded her hands. "We won't stay for too long. We'll try to be gone by morning."

"Oh, no. You're a priestess. Stay as long as you need." With that, she turned and headed for the kitchen.

"Well," Yojackson said. "You get a lot of favors whenever you whip out that title, priestess."

"And see what being a pirate gets you?" She crossed her arms.

He merely smirked. "So, since I'm clearly the head of this outfit, looks like I'm up first for the bath."

"Well, Aome is the priestess," said Rynn mischievously. "She has the title. She should get to bathe first."

"You're a celestial child."

"You're my escort." He raised his eyebrows at her.

Yojackson frowned as Aome shrugged playfully and skirted him before shutting the door in front of him. "Well then." He folded his arms.

Kilderan stepped towards him and muttered, "You almost gave us away back there. You almost used your real name."

"Please, these people are harmless. They wouldn't have called us in."

"They would have. Just try to be more careful. We can't have anyone who is associated with the emperor know about us, especially when we're so close to Thruhairth." Kilderan turned toward Rynn and beckoned him to his side, and they deserted Yojackson.

Once they were in the main area of the house, Kilderan went to the window and stared out at the meadow, though Rynn could not see anything in the darkness for him to gaze at.

The aroma of herbs and spices filled Rynn's nose once more and he glanced at the crude counter where Iva prepared the food. He leaned against the table and fiddled with his sleeves.

Within a few moments, Aome was already out of the bathroom and wearing a pale blue dress with a skirt and sleeves as puffed up as Iva's. Her hair was still wet and some of it clung to her forehead.

Rynn and Kilderan studied her, having never seen the priestess in any sort of dress. Yojackson scrutinized her.

"Oh! Lovely!" Iva threw her hands in the air and stepped towards Aome. "A little loose, but other than that it fits you wonderfully!" She leaned closer to Aome and winked. "I was afraid it wouldn't work."

"Yes, it's very comfortable, thank you." She smoothed the skirts and then took Kilderan's place by the window as the young man left to bathe.

"Where is Koto?" Rynn asked.

"Probably out in the meadow with the jungov," Iva replied without shifting her attention from the maroon tuber she was slicing.

Rynn stepped out of the small house and into the crisp night air. There was a pale indigo light from the sky that partially illuminated his path. He soon spotted Koto leaning against a wooden fence. He waded through the tall grass and wildflowers, soon coming to the old man's side.

Neither one of them said anything, and Rynn stared at the large creature that seemed both amphibious and bovine as it trudged around its spacious pen and clawed at the ground lazily.

"I like your farm," Rynn told Koto.

He turned to the boy. "Is that so?"

Rynn nodded. "It's very…quiet." *It reminds me of home.*

Koto leaned on one arm. "Say, son, where do you and your friends come from, anyway?"

"Oh. Um. We're just traveling. We've come from the city," he lied. *But it isn't completely a lie…*

Koto raised his eyebrows, and Rynn could not tell if he was merely expressing a small degree of interest or if the old man did not believe him.

"Who is the young man with…with the long hair and the blue eyes?" As he said this, he made motions with his hands towards his own hair and eyes.

"He's my brother." Rynn smiled. *My brother.*

"And who is the other man?"

"My friend."

"They seem vaguely familiar, for some reason. Like I've seen them somewhere. Never seen your face before, though." He squinted and grinned at Rynn.

The bounties on Kilderan and Yojackson's heads. Rynn grew uneasy. "Um. I—I should go back inside and check on my brother, actually."

Koto looked as if he was about to say something, but he instead turned his attention back to the jungov.

Rynn rushed back to the house once Koto had faced away, feeling anxious. *I need to find Kilderan.*

Iva said something to him on his way past, but in his haste he ignored the old woman as well as Aome and Yojackson, who were talking with her. The hall was dark, and a blue beam of moonlight flooded from the bathroom onto the floor in front of Rynn. The scent of warm, soapy water wafted past.

He found Kilderan, facing a slightly foggy mirror and precariously putting down a knife he had been holding up to his clump of wet hair before unfolding a gray blouse, his body stiff.

They both jumped. Kilderan, because Rynn stepped on a loose, creaky part of the floor, shattering the silence, and Rynn because he saw that Kilderan's bare back was covered in an array of silvery scars and faint purple bruises. Rynn stared at the wounds for a second longer before Kilderan spun around to face him, gripping the tall dresser behind him to support his wounded leg. There were even more scars and bruises on his torso, from which his ribs slightly protruded, including an array of peculiar round scars scattered across his abdomen.

Rynn frowned as he studied his brother. He then noticed a blood red crystal hanging like a pendant around his neck and gazed at it for a heartbeat.

"Rynn? What's wrong?" At the same time, Kilderan was gingerly tugging the shirt over his head. He seemed aware of Rynn gaping at his wounds.

Rynn had forgotten whatever it was that had caused him to rush to Kilderan for. He remembered the bruises he had seen on Kilderan's arms during one of the nights on Yojackson's ship. He was confused and disturbed. His mind became a void. "I don't know. There was something I needed to tell you but…I forgot."

Kilderan blinked a few times, droplets of water clinging to his dark eyelashes. His shirt became soaked by his hair laying on it. He limped over to the large, neatly made bed and seated himself, wincing. "All right." He leaned back slightly. "Rynn, listen to me-"

"Hey, um…"

Both of their heads snapped up and they turned to the doorway, where Yojackson leaned.

"I don't want to interrupt your moment, but we need a plan." He stepped across the old wooden floor and joined Rynn where he stood.

"What?" Kilderan asked absently.

"For finding Velle Deka." He turned to see Aome slipping into the spare bedroom as well. "That's what we're trying to do, isn't it?"

"Of course it is," Kilderan retorted.

It was a moment before Aome said, "The high priestess retreated to our designated safe place below the city, where it is very difficult to be picked up by trackers or the like. We should head there."

"And you know exactly where this is?" Kilderan asked, wringing his hands.

Aome nodded. "All of the priestesses do." A second later, she corrected solemnly, "Did."

Yojackson glanced at her.

"In the morning. We'll leave," said Kilderan.

"That's not a plan!" Yojackson protested. He groaned. "Now I'm sounding like Aome."

"You *do* know my name." She cocked an eyebrow at him.

"I never had a plan. I never needed one. I only ever had to get Rynn away and safe." Kilderan folded his arms and frowned at Yojackson.

"What happened to the fact that we're kind of"—here he lowered his voice—"on the run?"

"We're safer here than we are in Thruhairth."

"Well—"

"Can you please stop arguing?" Rynn pleaded. He yawned. "We sort of have a plan. Aome's going to take us to the safe place."

Kilderan dropped his gaze to the floor. "Just...all of you...I think the food's ready."

• • •

Rynn and Kilderan were silent as they all sat around the table, Rynn searching his mind for the information he knew had to be important. Yojackson and Aome were talking with Koto and Iva, but Rynn's thoughts were so far from the little farm that he barely heard them. He picked at the roasted toad that was stuffed with vegetables and bread crumbs, not hungry any longer after seeing Kilderan's bruises. His fingertips buzzed and he grew disturbed, feeling that Kilderan in actuality had not divulged anything to him. He wondered where his brother had really come from.

He suddenly yawned, and Kilderan announced to the table, "We're leaving in the morning. We should rest."

Aome thanked Iva before they all stole away to the room offered to them.

Rynn could hardly see in the darkness, and stumbled around before colliding with Kilderan. His brother gripped his shoulders to steady him. "Are you feeling all right?"

Rynn scratched his head. "Yeah. There was just...there was something I needed to tell you, something really important. But I forgot."

Kilderan began to turn away.

"Something really, really important," Rynn insisted. He thought for a moment. "Something about Koto."

"I know. They look at me a little suspiciously."

Rynn furrowed his brow and bit his lip, trying to think. He yawned again.

•••

Rynn watched from beneath the thin quilts as Kilderan shifted near the window. He could not make out his brother's face, for the moonlight had grown sparse. He yawned again and rolled onto his side, balling the corner of the blanket up in one of his fists. Images came to his mind, of Kazari's burning temple and of Asold being stabbed and of Kilderan, masked, first gazing upon him when he hid in the closet. His cheeks were flushed and his arms throbbed. It was as if the blood wanted to escape his veins and cascade over the side of the wooden bed frame and its clean white sheets and pool on the rickety floor.

Rynn shut his eyes, the last image before the blackness being one of his shining blood flowing from his arm.

The suns did not allow him to open his eyes easily the following morning, for their bright, cheerful beams fell right into his face. Rynn yawned and rubbed one of his eyes, not opening them yet.

The bounties on Kilderan and Yojackson's heads!

He suddenly sat upright and everyone who had been peacefully slumbering stirred, except for Kilderan, who nearly leapt from his pile of quilts. His hair was tangled and he blinked at Rynn. "Are you all right?"

"I just remembered what I was going to tell you," Rynn breathed.

"Slow down. What is it?"

Yojackson reluctantly left his makeshift bed on the floor to don his long maroon jacket over the cream-colored tunic he wore. Aome pulled on her own jacket, having changed into her original outfit, and then moved from her own bedding arrangement to the cushioned chair by the window and looked at Rynn and Kilderan with a questioning look.

"Koto said that you and Yojackson looked familiar. I think he was talking about the bounties."

"Woah, keep it down, blast it!" Yojackson whispered. "I haven't been free this long by announcing it to everyone from here to Ganymede."

Aome gave him a look.

"The bounties?" Kilderan turned to Yojackson. "We have to get out of here. If there's any chance that they know who we are, we could get caught. Quick, get dressed."

"You're afraid of an old farmer and his wife," Yojackson said, eyebrows raised.

"Koto seemed suspicious," Rynn put in.

"How suspicious?" Kilderan asked.

Rynn shrugged, recalling his talk with Koto by the jungov pen. "He pressed me with questions about you, and you," he gestured towards Yojackson.

"Kilderan's right," Aome said. "We should leave. Koto and Iva are a nice couple, but we shouldn't trust anyone too readily." She stared down at her folded hands before adding, "We need to head for the safe place."

Kilderan gingerly stood with a wobble and made his way to the doorway, limping.

"You didn't remove that bullet correctly," Aome muttered to Yojackson.

"You've said that before. Would you rather have had him bleed out?"

She did not respond and instead joined Kilderan in leaving the room, as did Rynn.

Rynn was greeted by Iva as soon as he left the hallway and entered the main part of the cottage, which looked bright and friendly in the morning sunlight.

"Ah! I have something for you, Rynn." She stood, leaving a plate of half-eaten fruit and slices of meat. "Now stay here for a moment." She adjusted the apron around her waist and left the cottage.

Rynn glanced at the others, confused.

When Iva returned, she had a large basket of clothing and sheets in her arms. On top of the pile was Rynn's long, loose white tunic.

"I fixed the sleeves for you," the old woman said, holding the shirt up for Rynn to view. She smiled, delighted. "I noticed that they were far too long for a child."

Rynn studied the sleeves, which were cuffed, making them much shorter. They were stitched back by ink-colored thread.

"Oh, the thread," Iva said. "I was out of white. I hope you don't mind."

"No, not at all." He smiled at her. "Thanks. Those sleeves really were getting annoying."

Iva smiled at him. She noticed the three adults standing behind him. "Oh. I have breakfast on the counter. Koto is out with the jungov."

"Thank you," Aome told her, "But we have somewhere we need to be. You and Koto letting us stay here really was appreciated."

"Ah, anything for a celestial priestess. It's the least we can do. Goodbye, then. Stay safe." With that, she turned back to the laundry basket and set it on the old table, starting to fold the clothes it held.

Aome looked at Yojackson and Kilderan, and they left the quiet cottage. It felt to Rynn like they had stayed there for years rather than one night. The knowledge that they would likely face more trouble as soon as they were out of the meadow made him reluctant to leave, but he fell in beside Kilderan anyway.

XVII

The smell of smoke was thick in Rynn's nose and his eyes were stung by the remaining cinders that drifted through the air, carried by the wind. His footsteps were soft on the ground as he followed behind Aome as the priestess led them through the meadow close to Kazari's temple.

She turned back to him. "We'll be there soon."

"You're taking us back to the temple?" Yojackson asked, with a glance towards the place in the tall grass where they had parked his cycle. "We have a vehicle, you know."

"We should walk. Trust me," she said.

"But—"

"We're walking."

Rynn soon laid eyes on the wreckage of the destroyed temple, but rather than approaching the scorched shrine Aome wove through the white flowers where the meadow continued behind the temple.

A small garden stood before them, almost untouched by the fires that had ravaged the shrine. It was contained by an old metal fence but the gate acting as the entry was open, swinging on its hinges.

Aome exhaled, almost coughing from the odor of the smoke. "This way."

Soon the meadow was obscured on all sides as they stepped into the garden and were surrounded by fragrant roses and thick ivy, though the yard was well-maintained. Rynn glanced around, the pale pink flowers like delicate jewels in a verdurous crown.

He stepped aside, however, when he looked to his feet and saw the shards of a broken white pot with blue and yellow birds painted on it laying next to his ankle.

"I don't understand." Kilderan stepped towards Aome. "Why did you bring us to the temple garden?"

"Yeah," Yojackson joined. "I hate to break it to you, priestess, but I don't see any way we're getting to the hiding place from here."

Aome smiled. "That's the point." She raised a finger and pointed to the stone floor of the garden. "That is the way to the labyrinth. Through the floor."

"That's how the high priestess escaped so easily," Kilderan muttered.

"Yes, with her entourage. And they'll still be there when we reach the hiding place."

Aome walked over to the edge of the garden and knelt. After straining somewhat to lift the heavy stone, she revealed a large fissure in the ground. "Everyone down the stairs," she ordered. "Let's not waste any more time."

Yojackson was the first to slip past her and into the hole in the garden, soon disappearing into the darkness.

Kilderan followed a moment later, cautious because of his leg, and then Rynn, who felt Kilderan's unseen hand steady him.

Aome came last, but she then took the lead and immediately began walking.

"Uh…How far is this, really?" Yojackson glanced at a fork in the tunnel that Aome quickly passed.

"You wouldn't want the most secret location in all of Thruhairth to be easy to find, would you?"

"In our case, yes. Yes I would."

"Don't worry. I've never had to come down here before, but I know every tunnel."

"You've never been down here?" Kilderan asked. "Not once?"

"The celestial priestesses have been faced with the hostility of opposed citizens multiple times before, but something like an entire temple being destroyed has never happened," Aome explained with a distance in her tone.

"You're absolutely sure you know what you're talking about? This could be a huge waste of time," Yojackson reminded her.

"I've asked you multiple times, won't you just trust me?" Aome spun around to face him, impatient. She stood right in front of him and had to crane her neck to look him in the eyes. "No time where the celestial children are unable to be tracked is wasted time. Now *please*, can you allow me just one moment where you aren't questioning everything I say?"

"Whatever you say. I'm just here to help the celestial children." He smirked at her and stepped a little closer so that their chests touched. Aome stepped back. Yojackson ran a hand over his shaved head and adjusted his jacket with a glance back at Kilderan as Aome turned back around and trotted down the corridor.

• • •

Rynn did not know how long Aome had been leading the group through the network of complex tunnels, but his legs had grown tired and there was an echo that sounded every time a noise was made that had begun to annoy him. He would not ask her how much longer, however, because his entire journey with Kilderan had required patience and trust in strangers and he knew as soon as they found Velle Deka he was essentially saved. The thought shook him slightly.

"How much longer, priestess?" Yojackson asked, splitting the silence that had been looming over them for almost as long as they had been walking.

"Actually, we're here."

Aome halted in front of them and then turned to a wall.

Yojackson placed his hands on his hips. "Another secret entrance?"

She did not reply, instead knocking on the wall in a very precise rhythm that at different points required both pauses and rapid pounding. Rynn watched her for an agonizingly long time, and Yojackson muttered, "Isn't that a little inconvenient?"

Aome then stepped back and waited wordlessly.

There was no reply, no opening of the wall.

"Are you sure you've got the right wall?" Yojackson asked, though Rynn could not tell if he was joking or not.

A few heartbeats later, the wall slowly slid to one side, making a loud grinding noise as it did.

"You know, there's such a thing as scanners and chips and—"

"The high priestess didn't want to rely on technology for something like this."

As soon as the door had parted from the wall enough for Aome to fit through, she stepped inside, the others trailing behind.

"It's empty," she said, fear taking over her voice. She turned around to face them, frowning. "Why it is empty?"

"Sister?"

Aome's head snapped up as a woman who looked around her age who had intricately braided brown hair and a long white dress and cloak approached them.

"Lehn!"

The two women bowed to each other and then embraced. Afterwards they both stepped back and studied each other.

Lehn lifted a slender eyebrow. "Interesting replacement for your vestment, Aome."

Aome tucked a loose lock of hair behind her ear and smiled. "It's actually very practical. But I miss wearing the gown."

Lehn's expression grew somber and she said, "The temple was attacked. Every single priestess..."

Aome muttered, "I watched it burn."

Lehn suddenly embraced her again, cupping the back of Aome's pink braid and whispering, "I am so sorry, Aome. Really, I thought you were never coming back. But to be greeted by something like that..." She furrowed her brow. "Why *did* you return from your journey?"

Aome looked back at Kilderan. "It's the high priestess' entourage. They have to know."

"Sister, know what?"

Aome stepped towards Rynn and gently put her arm around him. "This is Rynn Hera."

"...Hera? You mean..."

Aome nodded.

Rynn's eyes widened as he glanced up at Aome.

Lehn slowly made her way over to the boy and knelt, holding his small hands in her delicate ones. The milky blue stone of the simple silver ring that she wore on her finger pressed into his skin. "The forbidden son," she breathed. "You are such a magnificent child, Rynn Hera. And you carry such a grave burden." She gave him a small smile.

"We need to see Mother Deka," Aome said as more of Velle Deka's entourage stepped out of the darkness and joined Lehn, who stood.

"Let me see your beads, Sister," Lehn said, releasing Rynn's hands holding out her palm.

Aome smiled at her, and Rynn could tell she was elated to be reunited with the remaining priestesses, her hieratic sisters. She pulled back her torn coat and reached for her wrist. Shock overtook her features. "They…They aren't here. My beads." She swallowed hard. "I must have lost them when I went in to rescue Tillie."

"Then you will not see the high priestess." Lehn had suddenly grown cold.

"But Lehn…You know who I am."

"And you know the creed. Even though we know who you are, we will not trust someone without the string of charms."

Aome glanced at Kilderan and Rynn, tears pooling in her eyes. She left Lehn's side and approached Kilderan. "I am so, so sorry. I have failed you."

"But…But we're here," Kilderan began. "The entourage is here. What do you mean you've failed?"

"Didn't you listen to her? Without the string of beads I always wear, I am not a celestial priestess."

"Wait." Yojackson shoved past Kilderan. "What do you mean? These people know who you are. Why won't they let you in to see the high priestess without some string of marbles?"

"It's not some string of marbles," Aome muttered, glaring at him. "Those beads are very symbolic as they are what mark me as one of Kazari's priestesses, as well as carry all of my identification." She ran a hand through her hair and dropped her gaze to the floor. "The temple has never trusted anyone. None of you would understand how strictly the priestesses must abide by the rules." She appeared disheartened.

Yojackson frowned. "How were you halfway across the galaxy, then?"

"Velle Deka sent me on a trip," she replied simply. She shut her eyes. "Without those beads, there really is nothing we can do to see her."

"That's ridiculous!" Yojackson raised his voice and stepped past her to stand before the high priestess' entourage. "Isn't there anything we can do to see the high priestess?"

Lehn shook her head.

"Can't you at least talk with her, and tell her that perhaps the rules don't apply when a celestial child who's in danger is involved?" He crossed his arms and his lips were pressed into a firm line.

Lehn glanced around at the other priestesses, and finally she said, looking at Rynn, "I will speak with Mother Deka." Yojackson was about to nod when she held up a pale finger. "Don't expect anything, however."

Yojackson unfolded his arms and returned to Aome's side.

As they waited for what felt like hours, Rynn watched her out of the corner of his eye, her expression neutral. Kilderan's breaths were steady, and Yojackson's jaw was clenched. Rynn adjusted his newly stitched shirt.

The priestesses who made up Velle Deka's entourage emerged from the blackness of the tunnel beyond where Rynn guessed the high priestess was hiding. Lehn adjusted a lock of her hair.

"Well?" Yojackson asked.

Lehn took in a tranquil breath. "The high priestess has agreed to see you."

Rynn's eyes widened, but he frowned as Lehn continued.

"Only if you will retrieve the necklace with a pendant depicting the three suns."

Kilderan glanced at Rynn and frowned. Rynn returned the look, puzzled.

"You want us to go after a piece of jewelry?" Yojackson asked tersely.

"Not any piece of jewelry. The item in question belonged to Mother Deka and it is of great importance to her, for only after it is in her possession will she be able to tell you what you need to know. She will not leave the tunnels, but if you will retrieve this necklace, she will see you. She is curious about the child."

Rynn felt pinned by her gaze, and shifted towards Kilderan, who Lehn then eyed charily.

"Where is this necklace?" Aome asked, her voice suddenly sounding reassured.

"The palace."

Kilderan recoiled. "Do you know what the emperor will do if he finds Rynn? Heading for the palace is the last thing we'll do."

"I am aware of the danger. That is why we're hiding out down here. But unless you somehow manage to find the beads, Aome, then unfortunately we will not be able to help you."

Aome turned to Rynn, Kilderan, and Yojackson, her eyes questioning.

Yojackson was the first to comment. "What kind of perverted deal is this?"

Aome gestured for him to lower his voice. "I told you, none of you will understand how seriously the priestesses take their creed. How seriously *I* take it. If we must go to the palace, then it is a risk I'm willing to take for the celestial child." She lowered her voice to add, "Both of them, actually."

"Wait. They don't know Kip has the blood too?" Yojackson furrowed his brow.

Kilderan shook his head. "No one outside of you three knows. I'd like to keep it that way."

Yojackson raised his eyebrows.

"But what about the palace?" Rynn queried. "We can't go in there."

Kilderan swallowed hard.

"I'll go," Aome offered. "I will sneak in and find Mother Deka's necklace. I won't come this far just to let you down, Rynn."

"All by yourself?" Rynn began to grow worried.

"No," Yojackson joined. "Not by herself."

Aome gave him a look, prompting him to continue.

"If you're going, I'm going. We can't split up this easily, not now." He glanced from Rynn to Kilderan.

"Really?" Aome asked, studying his features.

"You're planning on going undercover, sneaking into the most important building in the galaxy, and stealing priceless jewelry? Why *wouldn't* I come along for the ride?" He smirked.

A smile almost came to Aome's lips, but instead she exhaled a little impatiently. "All right. We'll go."

"We're staying behind," Kilderan put in, placing a hand on Rynn's shoulder, and Aome nodded. Kilderan glanced down at Rynn.

Aome made her way back over to Lehn and announced, "We will sneak into the palace for you and get Mother Deka's pendant."

Lehn bowed slightly before saying, "Thank you, Sister. Now, the necklace will be located in some sort of treasury or vault, and Mother Deka sent out this chip to gain access to it." She opened her palm and dropped a small green computer chip into Aome's palm.

Yojackson thrust his thumbs into his belt loops and, with a smile spreading across his features, said, "Well, priestess...Don't we have somewhere to be?"

Aome glanced up at him and nodded, her lips slightly curling into a smile this time.

XVIII

Aome had fastened her hair into a tight bun before mounting the cycle, but the wind that the racing bike created still tore at the few stray strands. She adjusted her hold on Yojackson's waist and stared down at the blurred ground beneath the cycle.

She worried about the celestial children, for she as a priestess felt some degree of responsibility for them. She worried, too, about where her sacerdotal beads had fallen off. Her bare wrist caused her discomfort, for the string of beads and charms was like the physical manifestation of her identity, marking who she was. She recounted every time she had been given a clay or glass bead or a charm bearing one of the celestial runes or some inscription. Her apprenticeship under Velle Deka had earned her first bead, and she recalled with some good-natured humor her first lessons, when she was younger and filled with endless eager questions about the goddesses, the true empresses.

She was pulled from her reverie by the criminal's voice, saying, "We're almost back to the city, priestess."

She said nothing, merely looking up at the hill on the horizon where the white palace sat beneath the slowly sinking suns, staring down at the capital city. A twinge of nervousness stirred within her. *If we fail at retrieving Mother Deka's necklace, then we fail entirely.* She frowned.

• • •

Soon Yojackson slowed the cycle as they came upon a cobblestone street lined with booths and storefronts that, even though nearing dusk, were already so swarmed with nobles and commoners alike that Aome wondered how they were going to make their way through the crowd.

They dismounted the cycle, and Aome placed a hand on her hip, gazing back at the distant shape of the palace, not as far as when they had been in the market, for Yojackson had brought them into the upper shopping district. "How do you propose we get in there? We can't just walk right up and expect them to let us in."

"Actually," Yojackson said, hoisting a bulging pack from the cycle, "That's precisely what we're going to do." He began to walk away, forcing her to follow him.

"What? What do you mean?"

He stopped in front of a shop with extravagant gowns in its window. "Well, lucky for us, the next few days the imperial court is open to every noble and aristocrat and highfalutin swindler who can find his way to Thruhairth."

"How is that lucky?" Aome asked, though she was already beginning to comprehend the pirate's audacious plan. "We aren't nobles."

"Ah, but they don't need to know that." Digging into the pouch on his shoulder, he produced a round green bag that was filled so that its drawstrings almost did not close. "We'll disguise ourselves." He tossed her the bag. "Now, go in there and buy yourself the nicest, prettiest dress you can find."

A smile broke across Aome's face before she smothered it. "Oh, but this is your money."

"And although I earned it in a somewhat questionable way, it should be spent on a noble cause. Now go, and I'll find something for myself at one of the less expensive shops." With that, he sauntered off, vanishing into the crowd.

Aome felt the pouch in her hands and smiled even as she shook her head. "Thank you, pirate." *Maybe you are some small degree of a gentleman.*

She stepped into the shop and started to study all of the bedazzled dresses and brocade robes and exquisite overcoats. She ran her fingers down the tulle skirt of a jade-colored gown, thinking of how she had never worn something so rich, being used to her simple white priestess gown and the jacket and breeches she had traded it for when Velle Deka sent her on a journey off of Arsteine.

"Can I help you find something?"

Aome's head snapped up and she glanced around the room to find a woman slightly shorter than herself standing near a counter.

"Oh. Yes, actually. I need something very, very nice to wear." When the woman peered at her, she held up the pouch and added, "I am willing to pay a lot for it."

The woman smiled and brushed back her bright orange hair, beginning to examine Aome as she stood there. "What kind of event is this?"

Aome thought for a moment, trying to invent a lie. "Ah…It's a…a banquet," she decided. "My…husband…and I were invited. By a few of Thruhairth's nobles."

Immediately the seamstress' face lit up. "Why, a lady! Why didn't you say so, Lady…"

"Yusef." *No one has a bounty on* my *head yet.*

"Lady Yusef!" The woman exclaimed. "Marvelous! Now let me see your eyes…Yes. Very lovely. I have a new gown that I made with a rare fabric just ordered from Zouel." As she stepped into a doorway, she added, "I think it will be perfect, Lady Yusef."

Aome tried to reassure herself that she had not broken the priestess' creed by lying, telling herself that it was for the good of both celestial children. Again she feared for their safety, and for what she counted as the thousandth time she was humbled by the fact that they trusted her as an escort.

The seamstress returned, carrying in her arms a bundle of sapphire blue fabric. She unfurled the gown and revealed it to Aome.

The priestess grinned. "May I try it on?"

The woman nodded. "Of course, Lady Yusef." She eyed Aome's bag of credits.

Aome followed the shopkeeper into the back room, where she was helped into the gown and then led back into the main area to a mirror surrounded by holograms of Arsteine's moons and the suns and jewelry that was on sale.

Aome took in the image granted to her by the mirror. The dress had a long, elegant skirt that hugged her hips slightly before spreading out, and her shoulders and upper chest were greatly exposed by the gown's neckline, though her modesty was preserved by the two joined sides of the dress over her bust. The sleeves were long and very large, though they clung tightly to her arms at her wrists. The seamstress turned her around and Aome saw that her entire back was completely exposed by the tasteful draping of the gown. The sapphire shade looked, in her opinion, magnificent against her fair skin and pink hair.

"It's as if it was made for you!"

Aome knew the woman only wanted to convince her to buy the ensemble, but the priestess felt that the gown truly was a perfect fit for her. "How much?"

"I would say, for a lady like yourself, twenty-two hundred credits. And I'll even throw in matching jewelry, no charge." The seamstress dusted her palms on her own delicately embroidered dress and bit her lip, waiting for Aome's reply.

Aome looked down at the plump pouch in her hand and remembered Yojackson's words. *...Buy yourself the nicest, prettiest dress you can find.* She smiled at the woman. "I'll take it."

The seamstress flashed her white teeth as Aome deposited the little bag into her hand to be counted and returned to the backroom to change.

A few moments later the shopkeeper returned with the gown in a protective bag. "That will cover the cost with one hundred credits left over."

"Thank you. Very much." *How much money did he make from whatever exploit he isn't telling me about?* she thought with some surprise as she took the dress and exited the store. *That is probably the most money I have ever spent in my entire life.*

• • •

After searching the streets for Yojackson, Aome soon discovered him lingering at a booth giving away samples of some gelatinous blue substance in small glasses. On his arm hung a sleeve similar to Aome's, likely holding his own disguise.

Aome suddenly felt guilty using all of his credits to purchase a dress she would only wear once. When he turned his head slightly, he noticed her and left the booth.

"Did you find something? I'm planning on sneaking into that palace very soon. I've been asking around and the imperial court is permitting the nobles in—"

"I spent all of your money," Aome blurted out.

Yojackson cocked an eyebrow at her and smirked. "Well, looks like we aren't as different as I thought, priestess." He slid up to her side.

Aome shifted. "Oh, I believe we are, pirate."

Yojackson shrugged.

"Now, what were you saying about the court of nobles?"

Yojackson planted his hands on his hips and leaned in, lowering his voice. "About thirty minutes. That's when they'll open the doors, and that's when we'll slip in undetected. I'm pretty sure I could pass for one of those high and mighty scoundrels."

"I would stick with just a scoundrel," Aome put in. "And how can you be so sure we'll be undetected? You may not remember, but you sort of have a bounty on your head. A bounty that may or may not be the largest bounty in the galaxy to date." She recoiled slightly when she realized the volume of her voice.

"What is with you and the kid? Try to act like you *don't* want me to get caught. I've been imprisoned maybe once or twice in my lifetime, and after the seventh time, it gets kind of old."

Aome raised her eyebrows. "Once or twice, and then you jump to seven times?"

He waved away the subject. "Just be ready to sneak in. We'll disguise ourselves in the back rooms of some shop, then head for the palace. Come on, I know somewhere."

• • •

"Won't we seem suspicious walking out of a bar dressed like royalty?" Aome asked as she stared up at the hologram acting as a sign over the tavern Yojackson had brought her to.

"Oh, it's no big deal. I come here all the time. And I'm planning on grabbing a drink while I'm at it."

Aome gave him a look.

The criminal and the priestess entered the tavern, which was smaller and cleaner than the one at Port Illuvar and more like a restaurant than a bar.

"Follow me," Yojackson muttered.

141

A few of the patrons glanced their way, but they went virtually unnoticed, even as they wove around all of the tables with their sumptuous disguises draped over their shoulders.

The back room of the tavern was very small and Aome found herself squeezed against Yojackson rather awkwardly.

"I only have a jacket," he said, "I can wear it over my usual clothes. I'll let you use the room." Before ducking out of the doorway, he said, "It's almost time, so hurry."

Aome stared after him for a half second before opening the bag containing the gown and dressing in the expensive outfit.

Once she was wearing it and had adjusted every draping of the rich fabric into its proper place, Aome found it difficult to maneuver out of the back door with the long skirts, though eventually she stepped out into the street and saw Yojackson standing around, waiting for her.

He gaped at her and the dress, and looked as if he was about to say something when Aome interrupted.

"Wait! The jewelry..." Using the pristine window of a shop, she donned the mass of sparkling crystals: the earrings, necklace, and bracelets, and she had twisted her hair into a whimsical braided hairstyle at the top of her head, also adorning it with crystals. She nodded to Yojackson.

"Wow. Spare no expense for the palace, huh?"

"Something like that." Aome's mouth fell open. "Wait. How do you plan on avoiding recognition?"

"Now's your chance," he said as a crowd of people dressed as richly as Aome swarmed the street suddenly. "Head for the palace. I'll catch up in a minute."

Aome furrowed her brow before turning and, lifting her skirts, hurried up the upsloping street with the aristocrats towards a waiting transport. She glanced back to where Yojackson had been standing, but the man was gone. She hugged herself, at the same time gripping the side of the large vehicle as it lurched and sped up the street towards the looming palace.

XIX

There was no sign of Yojackson for some time after the nobles' transport arrived at the entrance to the courtyard, and Aome grew nervous as the large ornate doors opened and a woman announced that the court was now welcoming Thruhairth's lords and ladies, as well as any visiting nobles.

Aome glanced around, squinting when she noticed a man who she believed to be the pirate she had traveled with all that time, but not entirely certain.

Yojackson trotted up to her, wearing an ornate, intricately embroidered long black coat and an elaborate hat, though he had not discarded his usual—stolen—jewelry. The scruffy facial hair that Aome was so used to seeing on him was gone, and he almost looked a bit younger.

She frowned slightly.

"Do you think they'll recognize me now? There's nothing I could do to hide my arresting good looks, but that's a risk we'll have to take."

He smirked, and Aome rolled her eyes, reassured that it was truly the flippant criminal hiding behind all of the gaudy disguises.

"Now," Yojackson whispered, "When we go in here, I think I know where the high priestess' entourage talked about, where they'd keep things like Velle Deka's necklace. I may have been in here before." He quickly leapt to a different topic. "Now, I am Lord Pyrrha and you have to act as my wife. The lord of Ganymede and I may have had a run-in a few years ago, so I like to think of this as payback." Aome was about to speak, and he held up a hand. "I already made certain: Lord Pyrrha has never come to Arsteine, so they won't be able to tell we're lying."

"That isn't what I was going to question," she snapped. "What do you mean you may have been here before? In the palace?"

He held up his hand and wriggled his fingers so that the diamond rings adorning them glinted in the sunlight. "Indeed I have, priestess. But contain your enthusiasm. There's a chance I sort of know my way around this place, but I wasn't in here long enough to get well acquainted with it." He smirked again. "But don't worry. I know what I'm doing."

"Of course you do." She suppressed a roll of her eyes. "Now keep your head down, just in case."

They slipped into the crowd of nobles being directed into the palace, and Aome heard a few of the aristocrats commenting on the emperor's rumored irresponsibility and carelessness. She, however, did not listen to the rumors, for her fundamental opinion of Emperor Dusek had been formed when she had seen Kazari's burning temple. Perhaps he really was reckless and running the galaxy terribly, but Aome only knew him as one thing: a monster. She had learned from Velle Deka how the emperor had truly come to power, and how he betrayed the true empresses, the celestial goddesses, thus explaining his desire to destroy Kazari's shrine.

Aome clenched her jaw as she remembered Sister Tillie and all of the corpses of her other sisters. But then she shook her head, clearing her mind, and faced ahead towards the massive palace doors.

"Hey! You, there!" someone called.

Aome glanced at Yojackson out of the corner of her eye, but the criminal-turned-nobleman's gaze was on the steps leading to the doors.

"You aren't allowed to come here! Step out of line this instant!"

Aome swallowed and dared to glance at the man who was shouting.

At the same moment, she exhaled, relieved. The armored guard was pulling someone who was far from her and Yojackson out of line, an ill-disguised commoner holding a pouch with something spilling out of it.

A commoner. Like her.

But Yojackson was who Aome worried for the most, for unlike her he had a bounty on his head issued by the emperor himself. She remembered Kilderan, and that he too was wanted everywhere in the galaxy. Aome wondered what he had done, as if being affiliated with Yojackson Owens was not enough.

Aome ended up a few feet in front of Yojackson, and she felt his eyes on her back. She forced her stiff shoulders to relax, realizing no one would believe she was who she claimed to be if she herself did not. Her skirts trailed behind her on the stone steps, and as soon as she stepped into the palace alongside the other summoned nobles, the smell of their expensive soap and flowery perfume and potent cologne filled her nose. She exhaled, one brief breath. The fresh air had faded away and now the smells of the nobles and their rich clothing and an altogether staid atmosphere came over the hall.

Yojackson was at her side, and he bent to her ear before listing his head and whispering, "The next corridor. That's when we split from this group."

She glanced up at him, the scent of his own cologne invading her nostrils.

"Trust me. I know my way around this place."

She blinked at him, in a way she hoped conveyed that she did not trust him.

The nobles were led along for another few steps before Yojackson and Aome attempted to step away from the group, but to no avail.

"Lord Pyrrha!"

Yojackson froze.

Aome turned, seeing that standing behind her was a stout man with strangely curled ears and a spine running down his head and neck and wearing a long velvet robe.

Yojackson's face became a mask of relaxation, to Aome's surprise.

The noble made his way over to Yojackson and said, "I have never met you or your wife before, though I have heard how well you preside over Ganymede. My name is Fregni, I'm a baron in charge of one of Arsteine's largest trade enterprises." He gave them a low bow.

"Ah!" Yojackson bowed and then spread his hands, acting as if he knew of this man. "Baron Fregni! I've also heard about what you've done for Arsteine, though I have never had the pleasure."

Fregni folded his hands in his sleeves. "I have to say, you aren't what I was expecting, but your wife is one of the loveliest noblewomen here."

Yojackson straightened and smiled at Aome, who tried to conceal how uncomfortable she was. "Yes, I'd say she is."

Aome's gaze flicked to Yojackson and her lips parted.

"You should come with me to my party's assigned chambers," Fregni said, pulling Aome from her daze. "We're going to have a meal while we wait on Emperor Dusek."

Yojackson furrowed his brow. "The emperor will be here today? Not only his court?"

Fregni chuckled. "Yes, he will. I'd count myself lucky that he is taking the time. I hear he has been obsessed with finding these two criminals lately, that Yojackson Owens man who has been wanted before, and a slightly younger fellow who no one recognizes."

Aome's eyes widened, and she glanced at Yojackson, but he did not look at her.

"I'm afraid I'll have to turn down your offer, Baron. The lady and I have…other plans."

Fregni's eyes lit up and he chuckled again. "Ah, I see. Well, I'll let you to it. I hope to see you at the conference."

Yojackson smiled and at the same time gestured for Aome to follow him away from the group, though two guards also split from the party and escorted them.

"I think we're good, gentlemen," Yojackson said to the guards.

"Anyone inside this palace is to be monitored at all times, for their safety and that of the emperor and his court," replied one guard, whose face was obscured and who carried a tall, menacing spear.

Yojackson frowned and glimpsed Aome out of the corner of his eye.

"Lord Pyrrha, is something wrong?" asked the other masked guard.

Yojackson glanced from the guards to Aome. Finally, he said, "No. Nothing is wrong."

Aome listed her head and they proceeded down the hall.

XX

The high priestess' entourage had not left Rynn and Kilderan as soon as Yojackson and Aome had deserted the tunnels, and Rynn felt that every pair of eyes relentlessly scanned him and Kilderan, who had seated himself in the corner and rested his arm on the knee of his uninjured leg. Rynn could see their plain white robes out of the corner of his eye, and he averted his gaze to the ground before it slowly crept along the stone floor and to the tip of Kilderan's black boot.

One of the priestesses shifted and cleared her throat. Rynn blinked, looking over his shoulder at Lehn.

"Can we offer you something to eat, Prince?"

Rynn shook his head, perturbed by the title she used for him. "You can just call me Rynn," he murmured. He creased his brow and said, louder, "You'll offer me food but you won't let us see Velle Deka?"

Lehn did not answer, and instead let her gaze drift from the young boy to his brother.

Rynn, too, glanced over at Kilderan, whose head was down, face obscured by his dark brown hair. His fingers twitched idly, Rynn guessed out of boredom. Aome and Yojackson had been gone for what to Rynn felt like hours, but he concluded that there was no way it was possible because his legs were not too tired of standing yet. However, he approached Kilderan, veins fizzing, and sunk to the ground beside his brother, careful not to brush against him.

Rynn stared at Kilderan's sleeve and mused about where the young man had really come from, for every time he saw Kilderan Rynn grew more and more certain that there was something, or multiple things, that he was not being told. He thought about the emperor, the man who wanted, *needed*, to hurt him and who Rynn was wary of, and the fact that he lived only a few rows of storefronts from where the child sat at that very moment.

"What will happen to me?" he blurted suddenly, startled by the sound of his own voice and the fact that his mind had not even gotten to think about the celestial spring before he randomly started talking.

Kilderan jerked his head up, his eyes possessing a queer tint in the dim lighting of the old tunnel. He stared at Rynn. "What?"

"When we reach the celestial spring, do you know what will really happen to me?" He felt a pang of fear strike his chest and frowned, dismayed.

"No, I don't know. Not every detail, at least." He brushed his hair back, revealing one of the delicate earrings dangling from his ears. He shifted even closer to Rynn and lowered his voice, briefly glancing up at the semicircle of priestesses, who were muttering amongst themselves with an occasional glance at the boy and his brother. "You will…" He seemed to search for the appropriate words. "You will be…separated…from this world, the world of flesh and—and blood." He peered into Rynn's widening brown eyes. "You will take on the form that was meant for you as a celestial being, and…" He thought for a moment. "You will drift amongst the stars and moons and suns and nebulas for all of eternity. Safe from the emperor." He seemed to whisper the last part, and mostly to himself. Then he added, "At least, that's what I've heard, what I've been told. And even that could be false."

Rynn stifled a wince. The prospect of eternity never ceased to frighten him, and he was not entirely convinced that he wanted to leave the physical world. He did not understand, and he was nervous because of that.

Kilderan clasped Rynn's hand. "Don't worry. If anything, the astral realm will be the most serene you will ever be in your entire life. And you'll be safe," he said again.

Rynn frowned but did not release Kilderan's fingers. "Are you sure that Velle Deka will tell us? That she'll even *know*?"

Kilderan shook his head. "Aome seemed confident, but…" He did not finish the sentence, for Lehn approached and her shadow fell across their faces.

The priestess squinted at Kilderan before softly smiling at Rynn. "Your friends will return soon enough. Mother Deka will be able to ease your consciousness."

Rynn swallowed and frowned at Kilderan.

"This is ridiculous," Kilderan snapped, lifting his face towards the priestess. "Why can't you just let us in to see the high priestess and save the trouble of Aome and Yojackson sneaking into the palace? You're putting a sister in danger for a piece of jewelry."

Rynn raised an eyebrow at Kilderan's sudden impatience.

"Without that piece of jewelry," Lehn joined, her tone now matching Kilderan's, "The high priestess cannot and will not tell you what you wish to know. Be patient. You have not known Aome as long as I have. Your friends will do fine."

Kilderan pressed his lips into a firm line, not convinced.

Rynn believed he was more concerned about receiving the information on the spring than Aome and Yojackson's safety, and he wet his lips and folded his knees to his chest, considering.

XXI

Aome had begun to doubt whatever idea Yojackson had for finding the high priestess' pendant, because they had been wandering around the palace with the two guards at their backs for ages.

Aome stepped forward and muttered to him, "When are we going to do something? We're wasting time here."

"Just trust me"—Aome had grown tired of hearing him say that—"We can't just hit and run. Not here."

Aome was going to remind him that hitting and running had been his answer every other time, but she held her tongue and smoothed the skirts of her gown. The faint flutter of her nerves served to increase her unease, but she squared her shoulders and lifted her chin, wondering who the woman was that the name Lady Pyrrha truly belonged to.

After a few more steps, Yojackson leaned close to her ear and whispered, "You're right. This isn't working. Just stay close, I have an idea."

Aome nodded and then turned in unison with Yojackson. The guards wordlessly followed them down another hall and Aome cast her gaze around at the pillars and ornate decoration once more, considering the fact that someone lived in this luxury every day.

• • •

Yojackson's pace quickened and Aome lifted a part of her long gown so she could keep up with him. Soon their speed increased to a trot.

"What are we doing?" she hissed.

Yojackson glanced at the guards, who were following behind at a speed only a little faster than their previous gait. "We're going to lose the guards," Yojackson replied.

Aome frowned up at him, unsure of his plan, but they turned into another long, sunlight-filled aisle and she glanced over her shoulder to see that the tall masked men were no longer right behind them.

Yojackson led her near a gap between the pillars and muttered, "I don't think they saw which hallway—"

Aome heard the click of boots against the marble floor, and at the same time felt herself being shoved against the wall between the pillars.

She blinked, taken aback, and then slowly turned her gaze to Yojackson, whose hands grasped her shoulders and pressed her to the wall and whose gray eyes were mere inches away from hers. His lips were parted and his breath came onto her skin as a relieved exhalation. Aome felt a blush crawl up her throat and onto her cheeks, but she did not believe the man noticed it.

"The guards," he whispered, a smirk slowly curling the tips of his mouth, "I think they suppose we went down the other hall."

Yojackson began to pull away from her, and Aome let her shoulders sink. The criminal placed his hands on his hips and was about to chuckle when Aome shushed him.

"We've lost them, you were right, now let's get to the treasury," Aome murmured.

"I *was* right," Yojackson repeated. "And you're having trouble trusting me." He turned and followed her, beginning to trot down the hall. "You'd think they'd have more guards in this place, or at least brighter ones."

"They probably do. You just can't see them," Aome said, looking around the opulent hallway. The entire corridor was filled with the golden light of the midday suns, and it touched every pillar and every drape and every painting. Aome's heels clicked on the marble floor. "I've never been inside the palace. It's magnificent."

"As long as we don't get caught."

She tilted her head wistfully. "I wonder, can you see the ocean from the balconies? Thruhairth is one big slope so I've never gotten a good view of the sea."

"Yes, you can, and it's lovely," Yojackson quickly muttered, looking distracted for a moment. He then relaxed and turned towards a corner. "This way."

Aome stopped suddenly. "Wait."

Yojackson turned back and then approached her.

Aome sighed. "We really shouldn't be doing this. We're going to get discovered and…and I'm just gonna say it. I don't really trust you. I'm sorry."

Yojackson dropped his gaze to the ground, and after a moment he said, "Remember why we're even here in the first place. We're here because there are two celestial children whose only assurance right now is the hope that we can accomplish our mission. You yourself have expressed how honored and how humbled you are to be able to serve the goddesses in some way. Well, believe it or not I'm actually quite honored as well. And not only to be traveling with the immortals. I am honored to be serving alongside a celestial priestess." He blinked when she looked into his eyes, the sun illuminating his face. "You asked me to trust you in the secret tunnels, and now I'm asking you to trust me here. Now, I've also had to offer my encouragement to Kilderan, and this is likely the last time I will ever give a speech like this again. It doesn't suit me." He then took Aome's smaller hand in his and swept his other arm behind his back, bowing in a melodramatic fashion. He placed a kiss on Aome's jewel-adorned hand, saying, "Now, Lady Pyrrha, shall we?" He smirked at her before turning and sauntering down the splendid hall of the palace, looking a bit ridiculous wearing such fine clothing.

Aome stared after him, the jewels dangling off of her head chinking against one another. She said nothing, but allowed herself a small smile.

• • •

"Where is this treasury, actually?"

"I thought you said you've been here before, to the exact treasury we're trying to locate. Why are you acting so worried?" Aome asked, glancing down the length of the third hallway they had searched for the treasure room in.

"I have been in here before. That's why I'm so worried. I got caught by the emperor himself—well, sort of. I never really saw him. And then I was sentenced to be hanged." Yojackson spun around and stared at her.

"And not even that could stop you?" Aome pursed her lips, trying to remind herself what he had asked her to do earlier. *Trust* me. Aome blinked. *Trust a pirate. A criminal. A liar and a thief and possibly a murderer.* She forced herself to avert her gaze from him.

"Come on, we need to find that necklace. We've kept Rynn and—" he lowered his voice. "We've kept *them* waiting long enough."

...And someone who could likely be more devoted to assisting the celestial children than I am. She gave him a small nod and said, "Yeah. Let's hurry."

They rounded another corner and Yojackson paused. Aome came to his side and stared down the long corridor, puzzled.

It was a dark hall, dimmer than any of the others. There were only four doors in the walls, two on either side.

Yojackson pointed with a ring-adorned finger into the darkness. "*That* is where I almost got captured." He swallowed. "But this is good. This means the treasury isn't far." He shifted his weight before launching into a trot again.

They made their way to a small hallway less elaborate than the others and Yojackson immediately rushed to a large door at its end.

"Do you still have that chip?" he asked Aome, at the same time extending his palm.

Aome slid her fingers into one of her sleeves and removed the key from its hiding place, giving it to Yojackson.

He spun around and began scanning for the door's lock.

"I wonder how Mother Deka even has this chip," Aome mused, mostly to herself.

"Hey, in situations like this one I don't ask questions," Yojackson put in, fiddling with the chip in an effort to have it accepted by the lock.

Aome frowned. "I wonder how she has jewelry in the palace."

"All right, here we are," Yojackson announced, straining slightly to pull the door open.

As they stepped inside the small, unlit room, Yojackson muttered to Aome, "Are you sure we can't take a little extra? Look at this stuff."

Aome glanced around the room, at the fine curtains and capes draped over old crates, and at the ornately carved wooden chests likely containing things of even more value, and then her eyes fell on a collection of dusty, slightly battered canvases leaning against the wall.

Curious, she made her way over to them and pulled one back, revealing the faded portrait on the other side. A chill ran through her.

The portrait depicted a breathtaking woman with wavy chestnut hair that perfectly framed her face, frigid blue eyes, an elegant indigo gown, and crystal jewelry all over her body. A dazzling crown made to look like the three suns and Arsteine's five moons sat atop her head.

"Empress Zelia," Aome whispered, gazing at the woman's stunning face and eyes that despite being bright seemed melancholy.

"What?" Yojackson approached her. "A celestial goddess," he muttered. "How can you tell it's Zelia, and not any of the others?"

"The eyes," Aome answered. "Kilderan's eyes." She continued to study the portrait. "She's gorgeous." Aome had never known what the goddesses' mortal forms were like, and she hardly believed the paintings still existed. She felt unusual staring at a woman who had been gone for so long, whose sons she was helping to save in her absence. She whispered something to the portrait, so silent she barely heard it herself, and then gingerly placed the canvas with the others.

Yojackson shifted and began wringing his hands. "Um. I think I found a jewelry stash, over here. It might have Velle Deka's pendant in it."

"Oh. Yes, of course," Aome said, clasping her hands together. "The true empresses!" she exclaimed. "Zelia is marvelous. Rynn and Kilderan's mother…" She sighed as Yojackson showed her to one of the many chests strewn about the treasury.

He opened it and allowed her to examine the contents, saying, "Do we even know what we're looking for?"

"I think I'll know which one it is," Aome assured him, rifling through crystal earrings and large emerald rings and ruby hair gems.

"That's encouraging," Yojackson rejoined.

"No. I'll know. Well, I *do* know." She lifted a silver chain from the pile of jewels and examined it. There was a pendant hanging from the chain, one made of ivory and rimmed with some intricately fashioned black metal. Carved into the ivory were the three suns. Aome nodded. "This is it."

"You don't want to look through any more chests first?" Yojackson frowned. "Just to be certain?"

"We already shouldn't be in here," she reminded him. "Now let's go."

"Ha," Yojackson said, crossing his arms. "That was too easy."

"Halt."

Aome and Yojackson stood in unison, and Aome clutched the necklace to her chest.

"Blast," Yojackson muttered.

The two guards they had abandoned earlier now stood in the doorway to the treasury with two other guards behind them.

"Lord Pyrrha, you are under arrest for trespassing on imperial property. The emperor will be alerted shortly."

Yojackson glanced at Aome. He glanced at the guards. He turned back to Aome. "Remember earlier where I said this wasn't a hit-and-run situation?"

Her lips puckered, and she gave him a confused look.

Yojackson pulled his pistol from beneath the flamboyant jacket and fired at the guards before grabbing Aome's hand and rushing between the stumbling men, who soon brandished their large spears and raced after them.

"Well," Yojackson said, "This is now a hit-and-run situation, priestess."

Aome could not help but admire his thinking, the fact that he wore his original garment and the pistol holsters beneath the disguise. She quickly released his hand and draped the necklace over her head and tucked the pendant into her bodice. "How are we going to get out of here without going through the entire palace and getting noticed?"

Yojackson frowned for a moment, thinking, and then said, "Just do what I do and don't say anything."

"What?" Aome recoiled from him, but obeyed as the pirate turned and sped towards two large, open doors that led them into a huge garden enclosed in glass.

The fragrance of the flowers and fruit trees and the sound of the fresh, bubbling fountain calmed Aome. The dying suns filled the private gardens with an orange tint.

Yojackson squared his shoulders as they ran and Aome began to run out of breath. She glanced behind them at their pursuers.

The man aimed the pistol at the glass wall before them and fired in rapid succession.

"Okay, Aome," Yojackson said. "Here's where you don't say anything and trust me."

The glass allowed them to charge at it and break the wall into a myriad of glinting shards.

Aome screamed as they collided with the glass.

XXII

Aome could not recall the fall from the garden, and her mind was muddled as she tumbled down the steep clover-covered hill that the glass-encased yard overlooked.

Her gown became tangled in her legs and when the vertigo subsided she fluttered her eyes open and found herself staring right into Yojackson's face, the tip of his nose touching hers.

The pirate blinked and then smirked. "Why, priestess—"

"We need to go. Now!" she interrupted, extricating herself from the criminal and quickly brushing a hand to her chest to assure herself that she still had Velle Deka's pendant.

The palace and a line of buildings were behind them, and ahead was the glaucous spine of the forest.

"Head for the trees!" Yojackson called, bolting for the woods and leaving Aome multiple feet behind him.

Amidst running, Aome kicked off her heels and was able to sprint towards the trees. She felt something cold drip onto the back of her exposed neck and blinked up at the sky, which was a strange mingling of winking stars and gray thunderclouds. The rain soon sprinkled the ground, though it lessened when they reached the woods.

Yojackson had slowed his speed slightly and then turned back to her. "How far do you suppose we are from the hiding place? My cycle is back in the city, so we have no way of getting back, at least not easily."

Aome thought for a moment before replying, "We should just run. Worry about finding an easy way later." She gestured to the horizon. "The hiding place is that way, I think."

Yojackson nodded and jerked his coat into place before squinting up at the rain that was beginning to increase.

They began to walk, the leaves crinkling beneath their feet.

He glanced back at the palace and then told her, "It won't be long before they come after us. ...Before the emperor knows about us."

Aome's thoughts halted but she continued to walk. "If they follow us they might see where the hiding place is."

Yojackson did not stop either as he answered, "We have to go back, though. Rynn and Kilderan are waiting for us. If we don't try to make it back to the hiding place, we have nowhere to go."

Aome agreed with him and they continued to trek through the small region of Thruhairth that was uninhabited.

•••

After a while, Yojackson spoke up. "So, what did that priestess you saved mean when she said Velle Deka was one of the only remaining maidservants?"

Aome tilted her head and a drop of rain slid down her jaw. "I…I don't know," she finally said. "I'm also not sure why Mother Deka's necklace was being stored in the palace treasury. But I suppose all that matters is that we have the pendant."

"Or what you think is the pendant," Yojackson countered. "How is that thing supposed to reveal where the celestial spring is, anyway? It seems like just a necklace to me."

"That's good. It could mean the information is well-hidden," Aome suggested.

"Or it's the wrong necklace and we were almost killed for nothing."

"Please, pirate, I'm sure you've emerged unshaken from situations far more dangerous than that." Aome looked over her shoulder at him.

Yojackson shrugged in a way that confirmed what Aome had said, and he was quiet for a heartbeat. "We're so close to saving that kid once and for all."

"Why do you sound relieved?" Aome lifted an eyebrow.

"Because this whole escapade has been nothing but close calls." He removed the hat that was part of his disguise and scratched his head. "But I sort of knew that coming into this."

Suddenly, Aome heard the rumble of a speeder in the distance and lifted her head. "Do you hear that?" she asked Yojackson. "I think there's a road up ahead."

Yojackson placed his hat back onto his head and they traipsed through the labyrinth of trees and thorns.

"Hey! Pyrrha!" a voice called when they reached the almost empty road.

Yojackson's head snapped up. "Baron Fregni!" he called with some caution in his tone. "What are you doing out here in the rain?"

"I could ask you the same thing. "Have you heard about the two disguised thieves in the palace? They're still on the loose."

"Wow. Really?" Yojackson scratched his head and feigned shock.

The baron leaned out of an electric blue speeder with a few other nobles seated in the back.

Yojackson glanced from Fregni to Aome. "Hey, um. We need to get somewhere. You wouldn't mind giving us a ride, would you?"

•••

The rain had lessened and the five moons had completely overwhelmed the suns by the time Fregni drove them into the shopping district and down the street where Yojackson had parked his own cycle.

They swiftly disembarked and Yojackson thanked Fregni, though he cast a nervous glance towards Aome.

"Hey, anything for a lord of an entire *planet*!" Fregni called, sounding impressed, before the speeder disappeared around a corner of shops.

Yojackson inclined his head and sighed, relieved. "That was close. Clearly, alerting the emperor takes longer than I thought."

"We still need to get out of here," Aome said as they climbed into the racing cycle. "Because as soon as Emperor Dusek knows you're so close, we'll be in even more trouble."

Yojackson nodded before awakening the cycle.

"...Why does Kilderan have a bounty on his head, do you know?" she asked.

Yojackson sighed, a quick, sharp breath. "Maybe someone saw us traveling together and word reached Dusek. I don't know. All I know is that he has a bounty, and that makes things worse for everybody."

Aome listed her head, only partly believing him, and wrapped her soaked arms around his waist as the cycle lurched before carrying them away from the capital far faster than it had taken them there.

XXIII

"I think they're in trouble, Kilderan," Rynn said, creasing his brow. "They've been gone an awfully long time."

"The high priestess' entourage never said this would be an easy job," Kilderan told him. "They'll be okay. Yojackson knows what he's doing."

Rynn nodded, but could not help the clenched feeling in his stomach. He hugged himself, and sort of wanted to hug Kilderan, but stuffed his hands under his arms instead. His veins pulsed as if they were about to short and the eyes of Lehn and the other priestesses did nothing to lessen his unease.

He could feel Kilderan staring at him, and he shifted.

"It's okay," his brother muttered. "They'll be okay, and soon you'll be okay. I truly believe they've found the pendant."

Rynn bit his lip, and his eyes were growing tired.

• • •

After what seemed like nearly an hour more, Lehn stepped towards him and was about to kneel to look him in the eye when everyone in the tunnel perked up at the sound of staggering, hurried footsteps reverberating throughout the stone corridor.

Kilderan stood abruptly and Rynn followed soon after, and he soon laid eyes on Yojackson and Aome, but then he squinted at them. Aome wore a stunning but soaking wet gown and Yojackson looked slightly unfamiliar, and soon Rynn realized it was because the stubble on his face was gone.

Kilderan gripped Yojackson by the shoulders and asked worriedly, "They didn't see you, did they?"

Yojackson shrugged. "You do know I'm a thief, right? It's part of the job description."

Aome gave the pirate a surprised look before smoothing her damp hair and smiling at Rynn.

Kilderan turned to the priestess. "The pendant. Did—did you get the pendant?" His breathing suddenly sounded more ragged than Yojackson and Aome's.

Aome nodded and lifted a chain up from her neck.

"That priestess had better let us in now," Yojackson said brusquely.

They returned to the circle of white-robed women and Aome removed the necklace, a silver chain holding an ivory pendant with a carving of the suns, and handed it to Lehn.

Lehn shook her head and closed Aome's hands around the pendant. "You should give it to Mother Deka yourself."

"You will still need a replacement set of beads," added one of the priestesses.

Aome nodded and glanced at Rynn, Kilderan, and Yojackson.

"I still think that was a little ridiculous," Yojackson said. "This is the celestial child we're talking about."

Kilderan listed his head towards Yojackson.

Lehn showed them to a dark curtain obscuring a passage through the wall, a path so narrow that they had to walk in single file.

Rynn felt Kilderan clutch his hand as they stepped into the darkness, but the pitch-black tunnel soon opened into a small, inviting room that was different from the foliage-covered stone brick walls where the entourage took refuge. The room, being scarcely used, was sparsely decorated with a few paintings of the suns and moons, a single cot, and a frayed yet vibrant rug. A satchel of torn, slightly charred scrolls was slumped against one wall.

A figure draped in white robes and a white cloak stared at the bare, sand-colored wall.

"Excuse me," Aome began.

The figure turned, lowering her hood, and faced them with burning gray eyes.

Rynn heard Kilderan shift behind him, and Rynn peered at the wrinkled face that somehow seemed as youthful as his. *Velle Deka.*

The End

Printed in Great Britain
by Amazon